ABSOLUTELY
AMAZING
FIVE-MINUTE
MYSTERIES

ABSOLUTELY AMAZING FIVE-MINUTE MYSTERIES

BY KEN WEBER

RUNNING PRESS
PHILADELPHIA · LONDON

9 8 7 6 5 4
Digit on the right indicates the number of this printing.

Library of Congress Control Number 2003095210
ISBN 0-7624-1772-2

Book design by Amanda Richmond

Originally published as *Armchair Detective 1*

This book may be ordered by mail from the publisher.
Please include $2.50 for postage and handling.
But try your bookstore first!

Running Press Book Publishers
125 South Twenty-second Street
Philadelphia, Pennsylvania 19103-4399

Visit us on the web!
www.runningpress.com

CONTENTS

UNSOLVED CASES

UNSOLVED CASES

—1—
SAFETY INSPECTION

If my mother is right and it's true that bad things always come in threes, then my day was down the tubes by midmorning already. To start with, I got to work late. Not my fault, but according to Mom the three bad things are never your fault; they just happen to you. Anyway, I got stuck in traffic on the Lion's Gate Bridge.

Arriving late meant that all the other inspectors had picked their assignments by the time I got in, so I got stuck with Ace Bagshaw. We have a new supervisor at the inspection branch, and he has this theory that first-come, first-pick will get the staff in early. It works, too. There's no way anybody would choose a Bagshaw construction site, yet we all knew someone would have to go to one today because of the carpenter who died there yesterday afternoon.

Let me tell you a bit about Ace. Of all the contractors the Workplace Safety Board deals with, Horace "Ace" Bagshaw is the only one who can make the entire inspection branch gag in unison. We're not exactly popular on a lot of construction sites, but he really hates the WSB. With Ace, putting one over on us—or on the works department or the hydro people, any government department—is like a duty! Doesn't help, either, that he's got this fat, red face with little piggy eyes and a gut you could park a car in. Anyway, that's Ace, so you can see why getting him on my duty sheet was the second bad thing of my day.

I got to the site at 10:05 that morning, just in time to be interrupted by the catering truck—which actually turned out to be a bit of a break. One thing you can be sure of at a construction job like this—it's a complete redo of a hundred-year-old house, three stories—is that a coffee wagon will draw in the entire work force. So from my car I got to eyeball the whole group. Five of them, including Ace. Should have been six, but yesterday afternoon a carpenter had pitched off a narrow ledge that ran along the front of the third story. He died in the ambulance.

According to my supervisor's phone interview with Ace last night, a proper safety rail was in place around the ledge, and, since nobody had seen the man fall, nobody really knew what happened. I could see the rail from my car. It appeared to be the right height. Just a single two-by-four about waist high, but that's all the safety code calls for. It was braced properly. Double-nailed, too: I could see the nail heads gleaming back at me in the sunlight.

What Ace had said to the supervisor was right, though. To make my measurements I'd have to go up through the inside of the house, and then crawl out one of the third-floor windows onto the ledge, just like the carpenter must have.

I got out of my car before coffee break ended. Might as well go present myself to Ace, I thought, and get the third bad thing over with. He didn't disappoint.

"Well, lookee here! Figgered one a' you people'd show up by now," he said before I had even opened my mouth. "What does a little girl like you know about construction? Yuh don't look old enough to tell a hammer from a pinch bar."

I forgot to mention that Ace doesn't like women, but that's

probably no surprise. In fact nothing he said was unexpected, but I must have been a bit tense, because I almost blew it right at the start.

"And where's your hard hat?" he bellowed. "This is a construction site! Don't yuh know any better?"

A really dumb move, but fortunately I still had my car door open, so I could swing around to get my hat in a manner that looked liked I always did it that way. Or so I hoped, but the smirks suggested I didn't quite carry it off. Ace, meanwhile, seemed to have accepted the inevitable.

"C'mon, let's get this over with," he said, running his hands up and down on either side of his enormous stomach. "I'll show yuh the ladders inside, and yuh can crawl up there on your own. See whatever yuh want. We're goin' back to work."

In my wildest dreams I wouldn't have expected Ace to climb the ladders with me, but it was reassuring to know I could go up without him.

"This job's been nothing but delay and delay." I noticed that he didn't look at me when he talked. "Sully—he's the guy that di— . . . fell? He put the rail up there hisself four weeks ago and two days work—two days—that's all we get in up there—on the whole job!—before that cursed strike. A month my equipment sits here and nobody works! Confounded unions! Then all that rain we had. Thank God that's over. And now Sully . . . fifteen years he's worked for me!"

Ace continued to mumble on about delays and the continuing problems of contractors as he walked away. I was glad to be free of him. Mounting the ladder, it occurred to me that I'd have to talk over the "bad things in threes" idea with Mom. I guess forgetting my hard hat was the third one, but I wonder if three things really count when you get one really good one in the middle. You see, even before I climbed the ladder, I knew I'd uncovered a huge safety violation.

Whether poor Sully died because of his own carelessness or because of Ace's probably won't come out till the inquest, but I know there was no rail there when he fell.

How does the WSB inspector know this?

—2—
THE BEST-LAID PLANS . . .

Linc Dennebar had planned every step of the robbery with great care, but killing Mary Majeski turned out to be more of a problem than he had anticipated. Not actually doing it; he'd rehearsed that part so often in his mind, the real thing was almost automatic. Mary's late husband had been a judge, and she kept his gavel on the mantelpiece. Linc simply took it and, with one blow to the back of her head, he . . . well, he knew from the way it felt that one swing was all that was needed. Exactly as he'd planned; she probably never even felt it. What he didn't expect; what he hadn't planned for, was the nausea, the wrench in his gut and the panic that overcame him when he looked at her lying so still on the floor in front of her wheelchair.

Later, when he was arrested, Linc realized it must have been the panic that led to his one big mistake. But at the time, when he called 9-1-1 on Mary's old rotary phone— the next step in his careful plan—the panic made him sound really genuine, even better than he'd practiced. Maybe too good, he thought. Might make the police get here faster, so it was a good thing he had the third step timed for speed.

That was to get the rings and bracelets into the hollow bottoms of his Nikes. He knew just which ones to take: Linc had learned all about heisting jewelry from an old con up at Rojax. That was the adult detention center where he'd done 180 days instead of at the juvenile house because some bleeding-heart social worker convinced the court that Rojax had the facilities to start him on a trade.

He'd learned a trade all right: the old con had even taught him how to fix the shoes, explaining how high-tech basketball footwear was the best thing that had happened to B&E since pawn shops.

Next, after pulling open all the drawers in the roll-top desk, along with a few cupboard doors in the tiny kitchen, and then breaking a glass at the sink, Linc had called Mr. Peevey back at the drug store, telling him about the horrible scene he had just walked into. This part of the plan was something Linc had worked on very carefully.

For the past several years, long before Linc came on the scene, Mary had been getting her medications delivered from Mr. Peevey's pharmacy on Thursdays—Thursday afternoons. That was an important coincidence, because the people in two of the other apartments in the little brownstone were always at work then. Linc had taken a while to confirm this after he had first seen Mary put the jewelry into the roll-top. As for the one remaining apartment, it was empty for the month, as the couple renting it was away on a summer vacation.

The other part of the Peevey Plan—he liked calling it that—was the delay strategy. Mr. Peevey knew how long it took to get to Mary Majeski's and back, but Linc had been stretching that a bit each time, telling Peevey that the old lady always seemed to have a bit of fetch and carry to ask of him when he showed up with her weekly package. The druggist didn't seem to mind that. She was a long-time, faithful customer, and good public behavior like that sure wouldn't harm the business if he ever needed to call attention to it.

Linc had wondered how he'd keep the call short—Mr. Peevey was a talker and would want all kinds of detail, but, again, being genuinely upset made it easy to just hang up.

After the call to his boss, there were still crucial things left to do. First, Linc pushed over a chair and jolted a knick-knack table off its accustomed site hard enough so that a cup and saucer fell to the rug. Yes, the rug. He almost forgot about that! Linc took a big, firm cushion and wiped out his Nike tracks, leaving those areas where they'd be reasonably expected.

Finally, he went out into the main hallway, closed the door, then forced it open with a screwdriver. This would be the final, clear indication of a B&E, the cap to his story: Linc Dennebar, delivery boy for Peevey's Pharmacy, arrives at Mary Majeski's apartment same as always; sees the open door; sees the old lady on the floor; calls the police. Straight and simple.

By now he could hear a siren—then two. Linc sprinted to the back of the hallway, secretly blessing old buildings, and dropped the screwdriver down a cold air register. Moving quickly, for the sirens were coming from the street below now, he pulled off the surgical gloves he had been careful to wear the whole time, stuffed them down after the screwdriver, and sprinted back to the door. Here, he hesitated for several long and agonizing seconds. This was a part of the plan that he had never been able to finalize with confidence. Should he wait for the cops at the door? Too cool. Go to the top of the stairs and shout? They might shoot him! Run down the stairs to the street? A lit-

THE BEST-LAID PLANS . . .

tle too freaked out. Or should he stay in the apartment with old Mary? Might look loyal and concerned, but . . .

At the last second he opted for running down the stairs. It would look better, he figured. "Upstairs! Quick, quick!" he yelled.

What was Linc Dennebar's one big mistake?

—3—
RECOVERY AT DUSK

The place was easy to find. After all, a pink-stucco villa in the middle of a rainforest is not easy to hide. Not that Selim and his band of cutthroats would even have tried to hide, for in this remote part of Sumatra they were in total control. What had been difficult, however, was getting to it. And getting to it unseen. Salah Selim and his people used a helicopter. There was a landing strip, too, for fixed wing aircraft, but Stan Livy and his recovery team had to come in the hard way, first by boat and then on foot.

They'd done it, though. Two days on the river and then a week of slashing through the undergrowth had brought them to the opposite edge of the valley, where they had hidden all day with binoculars fixed on the villa. Now getting out. That would be a different story! On the way out, they'd have the little girl with them, assuming the recovery went well. Timing would be crucial. On the way in, there had been some stretch to allow for things to go wrong, things that escaped their careful planning. But on the way out, they had to coordinate with the aircraft that would pick them up.

Be that as it may, Stan Livy thought to himself, that was then. This was now and, so far, everything had gone without a hitch. He was certain they had come in undetected. The four of them took turns all day watching what they could see of the activity at the villa and Stan had concluded that everything was what he called "site-normal." With the exception of one new member, this team had worked together many times recovering kidnap victims, and they could tell when a site was anticipating a rescue. Stan, in particular, had studied the villa with great care through the glasses. He'd wanted desperately to get closer, but a single glance from the valley side where the team had stationed itself made it clear that they dared take only one chance to get close, and that would be when they went in to recover.

Yes. So far without a hitch. Stan didn't like thinking that way, for overconfidence could jinx an operation. Still, it had gone smoothly. The new team member, the Dutch woman who spoke such precise, textbook English, had worked out just fine. She'd paddled against the current and hacked at the vines as hard as any of them without a sign of slacking. And her presence was a huge benefit. Crucial, in fact, for she had actually spent time at the villa working as a domestic, undercover for the Indonesian police. More important, her information was proving very accurate.

"The security system," she'd told them before jump-off back in Jakarta, "is comprehensive, but it can be penetrated. The compound is surrounded by a masonry wall, as you might expect, on top of which are motion-response cameras and barbed wire. The wire is electrified at key points—around the generator, for example. Guard patrols are somewhat haphazard during the day. After dark, however, they're frequent and regular. No one has ever tried to breach the security, and Selim has no reason to believe that anyone ever will. For all intents and purposes, he is the warlord in that part of the island. That might explain why he has the girl there instead of out in the rainforest, where he keeps the businessmen he takes for ransom."

Stan looked up at the sky and then back over his shoulder. Although the day still had enough brightness to hold the compound in its fading light, the jungle growth behind him was now completely dark. At this moment he was within a two-second dash of one of the entrance gates in the wall. The team had crossed the valley at early dusk, and everyone was in place. Getting close had worried Stan considerably, but, like everything else, the approach had been smooth as silk. What had concerned him most, naturally, was being seen, and for just a second his stomach had lurched when the sound of a horse's hooves came from along the wall to his left as he reached his pre-planned spot. It was not a guard, though, but an old man on what looked like an even older pony, accompanied by a pair of scrawny dogs. The quartet plodded slowly across the road that led out the gate, and on down along the wall.

Stan keyed a button twice on his handheld radio and whispered, "Sully! The noise coming at you! Not security. Repeat, not security!" Then he keyed the button once and whispered, "We're go! On my signal. Wait for it!"

He looked over his shoulder again, then rose slowly to his knees, one eye on the camera above the gate to see if it was picking him up but it was pointed across the valley. For a second he wondered if it could have . . . no, not possible; they'd kept well hidden in the trees. He looked one more time at the ink sketch on the back of his hand, where the Dutch woman had drawn a layout of the villa. With his right index finger, he stroked the pair of stun grenades clipped to his vest, and with his thumb checked the Uzi. He took a deep breath, waiting for just a bit more adrenaline. It was time.

That brief pause, as it turned out, was what saved Stan and made him call off the operation, for in that pair of seconds he realized that for the first time in the operation—the first time he knew of—there was a hitch.

Stan Livy has become aware that something is not as it should be, and therefore calls off the operation. What is the "hitch" he discovers?

—4—
CLOSING IN ON THE HACKER

The argument around the table was turning hot. The majority of the ICS team was confident they had identified the hacker, and wanted to arrest him, but Tara Kiniski was holding out. That mattered, because Tara headed up the team. Technically, hers was only a temporary appointment, for the simple reason that the team itself was temporary. The International Computer Security group had been put together by the RCMP two years before, when the World Trade Organization and the Canadian government announced that the next WTO conference would be held in Quebec.

As its title suggested, the team was in charge of computer security for the conference, and almost right away there was more work than they could handle.

Even before Tara had gathered all the code-slingers and chip-jocks and various geeks (from day one they'd been called the Geek Squad) she felt she needed—in fact, even before there was really any useful information to hack into—their own system had been penetrated. Nobody on the team, even the non-computer types, was surprised when it happened. Devoted hackers spend ten to twelve hours a day and more, seven days a week, trying to score in this way, so it made sense that someone might get in at the early stages. But at least the penetration convinced Tara's superiors that the off-the-shelf software set up to communicate across thirty-seven different countries came with firewalls that were next to useless, and that better defensive resources were necessary. It also made the ICS team more cautious, so when a tip came from the U.S. Secret Service some time later, they treated it seriously.

Because the American president would be attending the conference for two days, the Secret Service had immediately begun investigating every possible political opponent of the WTO. Almost as a reflex, the first one it looked at was "Randy Andy," Randalar Singh Anderjit, for he headed up an anti-free trade group that was regularly blamed, sometimes legitimately, for disrupting international conferences.

Everyone involved with the WTO expected interference from Randy Andy, but what had caught the interest of both the Secret Service and the ICS team was an unknown face, a long-haired, twenty-something male who showed up in photographs alongside Anderjit right after the Quebec conference was announced. A search of police records revealed that he was on the FBI's list of known hackers. A quick dig into some archived files identified him as an ex-student, first of McGill University in Montreal, where Randy Andy had studied, and then of Berkeley in California, expelled from both schools for allegedly hacking into their records and altering reams of data.

But for a bit of coincidence, this tip would not have merited more than the normal precautions from the ICS team, even though the subject, or at least, someone who was a dead ringer for him, was discovered to be renting a room in Quebec's Old Town area. However, on the very same day the advice came, Tara discovered that their system had been cracked yet again—not the original, weakly defended commercial system, but their new, super-secure one. Someone had managed to insert what she and her fellow geeks described as a "demon," a software program that operated on its own within their system. With this demon, and working through an anonymous server—probably in Bulgaria, Tara suspected, for that country was notorious in the cyberworld for such service—some hacker somewhere was now able to get into WTO files with an ordinary laptop.

Still, the news was not all bad, for Tara had a few shots of her own to take. Using a piece of hyper-trace software that she cobbled together herself, and with the help of the telephone company, she and the team discovered in less than twenty-four hours where that offending laptop was being used: the room in Old Town that the tip subject was renting! At that point, the "civilians"—the non-geeks—on the ICS team had swung into action. Within another twenty-four hours, they had a set of perfect fingerprints—"They're so good you'd think we'd taken him into a station and printed him!" Sergeant Proulx had said—and a full-time stakeout had been established in a house across the street.

But now there was a conflict. After a week of careful watching, the team, especially the civilians, wanted to have done with it and make an arrest.

"Look, we got him cold!" Sergeant Proulx insisted. "He's got to be the hacker 'cause your trace . . . er . . . er . . . trace thing or whatever, placed him. And the stakeouts, they're all saying he pounds away on the keyboard for hours and hours. This is the guy! Let's take him out! Then all you have to do is clean out that demon or whatever it is and we're in the clear! What are we waiting for? He's got to be the one!"

That sentiment echoed around the table emphatically enough to make Tara get to her feet when she replied.

"No. We just keep watching. I don't believe this guy is Randy Andy's buddy. Or even a hacker at all for that matter. I think he's a plant, set up to direct us away from the real one. If you re-examine the evidence and think about it for a minute, you'll agree."

Why does Tara Kiniski believe this is not the hacker the ICS team must catch?

—5—
A SAFE SHELTER?

The man lying on his stomach at the top of the ridge was named Tyl. In his village he had been known as Tyl the Miller, but his mill was gone now. So was his entire village. The Burgundians had burned it weeks before, just as they had razed every other village in their path as they marched through Flanders to the sea.

Tyl raised himself just enough to get a better look at the ruined building in the distance. He'd been watching it for hours, and his muscles protested the move. The Burgundians had been through here, too, he could see. What had once been a mill just like his was now part of a long, charred slash on the landscape. The mill was not completely destroyed, however, and that's what made it worth the long watch. It just might provide shelter for a while. Provided there were no Burgundians there—or worse, one of the roving gangs of bandits that followed in their wake. Even another wanderer like Tyl could be dangerous if he were bigger and stronger.

Tyl moved to his left, keeping behind the sparse brush that grew along the ridge. The new angle gave him a better view of the flock of pigeons that had made their home in the mill, and allowed him to look inside through a missing wall. The other walls still stood strongly enough to hold up the damaged roof, where the pigeons strutted so importantly. It was a wind-powered mill like most in Flanders and, while the vanes had been torn down, the tower was intact. There was enough of the building left, Tyl could see, to keep out wind and rain. The only problem: was anybody else there?

He sighed deeply and lowered his body to the ground again. He was weak, desperately weak, but his wife and their one surviving child hidden behind him in the trunk of a hollow tree were even worse off. Tyl was in his prime, if it could be called that, and had withstood the effects of starvation better than they.

The year was 1384, but Tyl didn't know that. It wouldn't have mattered to him if he had. For generations that year would be known throughout Flanders simply as "the time the Burgundians came." The previous year had been an even scarier marker. It was known as "the time with no summer" for, following a beautiful, promising spring, the rains had come and never left. The whole of Flanders, low-lying and flat to begin with, had turned into a sea of soggy mud. Creeks and canals had overflowed, crops had rotted in the fields, and people soon knew that famine was inevitable. By late fall they had begun to cast a reluctant, hungry eye at their animals. By mid-winter all the animals were gone. There was no hay or grain to feed them.

Tyl's village starved, but had done a bit better than most at first because one of the old women had convinced everyone early on to capture and breed the rats that seemed to multiply in times like these.

But when spring came, so did the Burgundians, determined to wreak bloody vengeance for having been kicked out of Flanders some decades before. The only good part was that they, too, and even the bandits, were having trouble finding food. Only yesterday, just in time to hide, Tyl's keen-eyed wife had spotted a troop on its way back to Burgundy, tired and bedraggled, the horses' ribs showing clearly through their skin.

A low roll of thunder brought Tyl back to the present, reminding him that even a ruined shelter would be better than a hollow tree for what was soon to come. He raised himself once more to look at the mill. Nothing had changed. On his hands and knees he backed away from the brush to collect his family. He looked at the sky. Although they needed to move carefully and keep to the trees alongside the stream, he calculated they would still have time to get to the mill before the storm hit.

Tyl has decided there is no one in the mill. What has led him to this conclusion?

—6—

MULE TRAIN

REPORT OF DISCIPLINARY ACTION

AGAINST: Trooper Zebulon Pike Hampton, 3rd Platoon, A Company, B Troop, 5th Cavalry

BY: Major Elliott Morton, OC, B Troop

CHARGE: Neglect of duty

DATE(S) OF OFFENSE: July 9, 1911

DATE OF ACTION: July 12, 1911

ACTION TAKEN: Thirty (30) days stockade, immediate

DESCRIPTION OF OFFENSE:

From July 2–10, 1911, A Company of B Troop was assigned to make extended patrols west of Flagstaff, Arizona Territory, in the area of three known smuggling routes (see Objective(s) of Unit). 3rd Platoon was given picket duty for the night of July 8/9, with Tpr. Hampton assigned to the most distant post from midnight to first light.

Tpr. Hampton failed to report a train of 20 to 25 mules that passed his post during this time.

OBJECTIVE(S) OF UNIT WHEN OFFENSE OCCURRED:

Effective February 28, 1911, and continuing as of this date, B Troop is posted to northern Arizona Territory, Sedona/ Flagstaff/Kingman area, to interdict smuggling of gold, copper, etc.

FACTS SUPPORTING CHARGE: (by Maj. Morton)

Tpr. Hampton was posted at the edge of a narrow ravine c. 0.5 mi. in length, and c. 100 ft. across at the widest point and c. 40 ft. at the narrowest. At no point is the ravine more than 20 ft. deep. The floor of the ravine is a mix of rock and sand, with a streambed that on July 8/9 was dry. The area above is thickly forested on both sides, so that to travel south with pack animals it is necessary to go through the ravine or detour some 30 mi. west.

The floor of the ravine was patrolled on July 8, and no evidence of recent activity was found. At first light on July 9, company scouts found clear evidence that a train of pack animals (mules)—approximately 20 to 25 animals, with at least four (possibly five) drivers—had passed through the ravine with hooves wrapped (likely in burlap) during the night while Tpr. Hampton was on picket duty. This evidence is verified and attested to by Capt. McNair of Company A (and Lts. Pocock and Nepp).

According to procedure, Company A was given a list of pack trains scheduled by the mines for passage through the area during the time of the extended patrol. None were scheduled for July 8/9, and none of the mines subsequently dispatched an unscheduled train on this date. These, in any case, would travel in daylight. The unreported pack train indicated in this charge, therefore, was illicit.

MITIGATING CIRCUMSTANCES:
(from oral deposition of Tpr. Hampton, as recorded by Maj. Morton. Tpr. Hampton is non-literate.)

Brisbois (Tpr. Brisbois, 3rd Platoon) was supposed to be on picket with me. There's always supposed to be two. But after about half an hour or so, he got sick and went to the cook tent and never come back. Nobody else come, neither, so I was alone.

It was pitch black that night and muggy. No moon, no stars. Couldn't see your hand in front of your face. Only a bit of wind, but it don't take much to make noise when it blows through all the trees, so you really couldn't hear nothing no matter how hard you tried. And anybody knows that if you work mules long and hard they generally won't make no braying sounds. Not like horses.

All I know is, if that pack train come through like they say, nobody could of known it.

COMMENT(S):

It is the conclusion of this officer that Tpr. Hampton either fell asleep at his post or abandoned it for a period. It is even possible, although there is no evidence, that he accepted a bribe. In any case, an alert trooper, at his post, in the conditions described above, would unquestionably have become aware of the passing of a mule train.

Major Elliott Morton, OC, B Troop

Major Morton knows there is something that would certainly have alerted the trooper to the passing of the mule train had he been alert and at his post. What is that?

7

WHY GRANNY DOESN'T RETIRE

Sometimes, at the end of a long day, Alice would agree that maybe her kids had a point, that maybe she should quit. Certainly she didn't need the money; Morty had left her with a portfolio that did a lot more than keep the wolf from the door. And she had to admit that all the traveling kept her away from the grandkids more than she liked.

Still, there were so many reasons to keep going. Like pride. She knew her children avoided telling their friends what she did—after all, how many seventy-two-year-olds make a living as a private eye? But the grandkids, they thought it was cool. She loved the look in their eyes when they showed off Granny Alice to their friends. And the truth is, every time she got close to the idea of packing it in, something would make her dig in her heels. Like that young snot at the attorney-general's department who wasn't going to renew her P.I. license because of her age. She'd put him in his place, because she knew the regulations said nothing about age limits.

Then there was the whole boredom thing. Alice had never been a back porch type to begin with. She couldn't sing, hated cruises, and sure wasn't going to be another blue-hair parked in front of the slots at Vegas. Morty always said she had a brown thumb, so gardening was out, and both bridge and golf she found dull. The action part was okay with those two, but for each minute of action, everybody spent another twenty prattling on about it.

All other reasons aside, however, the bottom line for

Alice was that she was very good at what she did. And being a granny gave her an edge. Take the case she was working on right now, the missing lady from California. From the interview this morning with the Mackilroy woman, Alice knew she'd found her. Well, maybe not in flesh and blood, but it was obvious this Torrey Mackilroy knew something.

"You and Pauline Ortona were best friends in high school, weren't you?" That was Alice's opening gambit with Torrey Mackilroy after showing her P.I. license. Torrey had been slow to answer, but that was natural enough. In Alice's long experience, everybody was edgy in a circumstance like this. All Torrey did was nod and then look at the telephone on her desk as though it might rescue her. Alice had anticipated—correctly, as it turned out—that the phone wouldn't interrupt them. She'd cased the place before and concluded that Torrey was a not-very-busy insurance agent in a not-very-busy insurance office.

"Pauline Ortona hasn't been seen in a very long while," was Alice's next move. "Her aunt, the one she went to live with in California when her mother died . . . she's convinced that Pauline's gone missing, but can't get the Santa Barbara police very interested, so that's where I come in. One thing I'm doing is canvassing all her friends, past and present, to find out where she might be. Naturally, you're high on my list."

Until then, Torrey Mackilroy hadn't said anything more than "yes," when asked her name. And all she had done in response to the "best friends in high school" question was nod. The nod gradually turned into a slow shaking back and forth when she was asked the whereabouts question.

"No idea," she said finally. "Sorry, none. The last time I saw or talked to Polly . . . I guess it's got to be . . . I don't know how many years now. Ever since we finished high school and she left Eugene to live in California. Her Mom died right after graduation, and . . . yes, I guess there were a couple of phone calls the first year or two. One letter, maybe. But nothing since I got married and moved here to Jackson and that was fifteen years ago."

She raised her head, looked straight at Alice. "Sorry, I can't help you," she said. She offered a polite lips-but-not-the-eyes smile and shook her head again.

Alice waited for more, but when the silence threatened to become awkward she put down her card with the usual "please call me if . . ." request and left. It was almost lunchtime and, although the interview had got her adrenaline up, she decided to have a salad at a nice, quiet restaurant she'd seen a few streets over. It had big tables, so she could take the yearbook in with her.

The yearbook: now there was a coup! Anybody could have done the interview she just did with Torrey, but getting the yearbook? Imagine some big, burly, male private eye doing what she did yesterday: going into James Polk High in Eugene, Oregon, breezing through the security, and talking that suspicious librarian into letting her take out their one and only copy of a yearbook! Grannies can do that, Alice knew. The sweet old lady shtick hadn't failed her yet.

She opened the yearbook to the page that had led her to

Torrey Mackilroy. She was Torrey Gallant then: "Better Known As: Tall T; Activities: Fashion Club, Student Council, Math Team; Favorite Saying: "You guys seen Polly?"; Usually Seen: Corner booth at Lubo's with Polly Ortona; Aim: Professional Designer; More Likely: Painting the booths at Lubo's."

Pauline Ortona's bio on the facing page showed a somewhat prettier girl. "Better Known As: Polly; Activities: Drama Club, Student Council, Cheerleader; Favorite Saying: "Hey, T, can I borrow your math notes?"; Usually Seen: Corner booth at Lubo's with Torrey Gallant; Aim: Actress; More Likely: Lubo's star waitress."

There were a number of notes and scratches and graffiti in the book that Alice had ignored at first, but a second run through turned up a pair of neatly drawn intertwined leaves, under which was written "TG–PO Buds Forever."

Looking over a too-large Greek salad at the photos of the two girls, Alice reflected on the phone call she'd made after the library visit. There were six Gallants in the Eugene book. Not only did she score on the second call, but Torrey's mother had filled in the blanks without missing a beat: "Yes, Torrey's my daughter. Name's Mackilroy now. Lives over in Jackson with her husband. They've two lovely young girls." And then, after some mutual exchange about the joys of grandchildren, Mrs. Gallant had freely supplied the necessary phone number and address.

"Now there. Let a young male P.I. try doing that on the telephone!" Alice caught herself, realizing she'd spoken out loud. Tapping her fork, too. She'd done that kind of thing quite a bit lately. Her ruse with Mrs. Gallant—it had worked before—was to pose as a volunteer for the alumni committee. And why wouldn't a sweet old lady be doing something like that? Quite simply, there were some things that seventy-two-year-old grannies could do far better than other investigators. The Ortona case was proving that fact yet again. No, Alice thought to herself, there were just too many good reasons to stay on the job.

"Now," she was speaking out loud again, loud enough to turn a few nearby heads in the restaurant, "now to get to work on Torrey and find out when she really last talked to Polly."

Why is Alice convinced that Torrey Mackilroy has talked to Pauline Ortona recently?

8

TRANSCRIPT: CROWN VS. JERGENS

TRANSCRIPT: CROWN VS. JERGENS, DAY 2

BAILIFF: All rise! Superior Court in and for the County of Grey is now in session,
Honorable Elmer Losch presiding.

LOSCH: Be seated. Mr. Weinert, are you ready? Your next witness?

HARRY WEINERT: Yes, Your Honor. The Crown calls Jack Scoles.

SCOLES SWORN.

WEINERT: Would you state your name and occupation, please?

SCOLES: John . . . er . . . Jack Scoles. I am a meteorologist with the government weather service.

WEINERT: Your Honor, the Crown is calling Mr. Scoles as an expert witness in this case and—

FRED BOETTGER: Begging Your Honor's pardon, the defense will stipulate as to Mr. Scoles's expertise. No point in taking more of the court's time.

LOSCH: Very well. Let the record show that counsel for the defense accepts the witness as an expert.

WEINERT: Just three questions, Mr. Scoles. Would you describe the weather conditions for the south of Grey County on August 20, 1941?

SCOLES: Records show completely clear skies for the day and night of the 20th. For the 21st and 22nd as well. Very warm. A day time high on the 20th of 89 degrees, low of

21. Sunrise at 6:18 A.M. Set at 8:11 P.M. Winds were . . .

WEINERT: That's really all we need for now, Mr. Scoles. Could you tell the court the moon phase for that date?

SCOLES: The moon was full.

WEINERT: A full moon. Now this is most important: based on your expert knowledge, once the sun has set, how much time passes before the moon in its full phase is completely visible above the horizon?

SCOLES: That depends on latitude, how far you are from the equator, and what kind of horizon, whether it's flat or hilly—a lot of factors. Here in the south end of Grey County, on a late August night—clear, of course— the moon is usually fully visible and giving off quite a bit of light after about one hour. Perhaps seventy minutes.

WEINERT: An hour or just a bit more. Thank you. No more questions.

BOETTGER: Defense waives, Your Honor.

LOSCH: Very well. Carry on, Mr. Weinert.

WEINERT: The Crown calls Mr. Jack Kaster.

KASTER SWORN.

WEINERT: Would you tell the court where you live, Mr. Kaster?

KASTER: In Neustadt. Northwest corner of Queen and Barbara. Bought 'er in '22 from—

WEINERT: Yes, thank you, sir. The northwest corner of Queen and Barbara. Now your home there has a porch facing west, is that correct?

KASTER: Yessir, west side. You see, the missus wanted a—

WEINERT: Just the porch, Mr. Kaster. Now, how many

other houses are there to the west of yours?

KASTER: None. We're the last—

WEINERT: And are there trees, say, a woodlot or bush to the west of you?

KASTER: Not a tree. Just Ed Demerling's big field 'tween us and the Hanover Road. I'd say she's maybe thirty acres. Ed, he's got wheat in 'er this year. Looks to me—

WEINERT: Yes, yes, could you tell the court where were you on the evening of August 20, 1941?

KASTER: Well, on the porch! Like I told you before, me and the missus were watchin' the sunset. You see –

WEINERT: The sunset. And is it correct that you remained on the porch for at least another two hours after that?

KASTER: Had to be about that. You see I went inside 'cause I wanted to hear the ten o'clock news on the radio, but it was already started when I turned it on.

WEINERT: Before you went inside—now this is important, Mr. Kaster—did you see a tractor traveling north on the road that runs along the other side of the field—I think you identified it as "Ed Demerling's field"?

KASTER: Yeah, the Hanover Road. Ten, fifteen minutes before we went inside, Art Jergens's tractor—

BETTGER: Objection!

LOSCH: Sustained.

WEINERT: Rather than say whose tractor it was, Mr. Kaster, could you describe—

KASTER: D'you want to know about the tractor or not? There's only one tractor for miles around here that's got this great big high bar what loops way up over the seat, and that's Art's!

BOETTGER: Your Honor!

LOSCH: A little more careful direction is in order, Mr. Weinert.

WEINERT: Yes, Your Honor. Now don't mention any names, Mr. Kaster. You saw a tractor traveling north on the Hanover Road and the tractor had a high bar that loops over the seat. Is that correct?

KASTER: Saw it clear as could be. See the full moon was just up and we could see it—what's that word you said in your office—sil . . . silhouetted? It was silhouetted perfectly against the moon. I even said to the missus—

WEINERT: And you saw this about ten or fifteen minutes before—

LOSCH: Excuse me, Mr. Weinert. Would you approach the bench? And Mr. Boettger?

CONFERENCE AT BENCH.

Note of Judge Losch:

In Crown vs. Jergens, the undersigned offered Crown opportunity to withdraw the charges against Jergens in light of Kaster's testimony, and it was accepted. Although the witness, Kaster, appears to have perjured himself, it is the view of the undersigned that the error in his testimony does not arise out of malice. There will be no further charges in this matter.

—Honorable Elmer Losch

What is the "error" in Kaster's testimony to which the judge refers?

—9—
"ODD BILLY" AND THE BACKPACK

Sharnell Yates made an elaborate fuss of pulling down the sun visor and adjusting it to keep the early morning sun out of her eyes. She fiddled even longer with the little portable radio taped onto the dash of Schomberg's sole police car. When the dial finally hit on the local weather report, she listened with head cocked to one side, as though it was the most important communication of her day.

What Sharnell was doing—and she freely admitted it to herself—was anything that would keep her from having to make small talk with "Odd Billy" Sniderman in the passenger seat beside her. Not that Billy was a chatterbox but he was unpredictable—and explosive. After two tours in Vietnam, "Odd Billy" Sniderman had come home to Schomberg with invisible wounds deep in his soul.

"The sun we've got this morning is going to stay right up there all by itself. No clouds, you lucky people," the radio host was saying. "Pretty much a repeat of yesterday. Good stiff breeze out of the west-southwest again, and that'll keep the humidity down, so you can really enjoy the day. High of 76 degrees, or if you're one of our listeners just over the border, that's about 23 Celsius and . . . "

"S'nother mile. Keep straight." Billy spoke for the first time since they'd left the town limits. He was sitting rigidly in the seat, eyes fixed on some vague point ahead of the car.

Sharnell nodded. "'Kay," she said, grateful for what appeared to be his calm. She wasn't really afraid, but there was no denying her uneasiness, and it made her miss the rest of the weather report. Billy had never actually harmed anyone, to her knowledge, or done anything blatantly illegal, at least by Schomberg standards. A larger community might have charged him with vagrancy, or perhaps found reason by now to force him into a treatment program, but small towns can be quite accepting of strange behavior, especially from one of their own. That was pretty much the case with Billy.

There was no question he'd earned his nickname. "Odd Billy" was often seen holding animated conversations with unseen companions. The look in his eyes was, well, scary, a feature that somehow seemed a bit more frightening because of his tendency to suddenly appear behind people without making a sound. No one, it seemed, ever heard him coming. Then there was his persistent habit of going into the stores on Main Street through the back door; in Schomberg, where nobody used locks in the daytime, that was easy to do. Perhaps the oddest thing about "Odd Billy" was the expression on his face. Sharnell had known him more than thirty years and had never once seen it change.

He spoke once more, again without moving. "Loggin' road runs off to the right after those trees up there. 'At's where you turn."

Sharnell could see the road he was referring to, and turned onto it a few seconds later.

"What were you doing way up here yesterday, Billy?" she asked.

"Walkin'."

She was going to ask why, but thought better of it. He'd

already agreed to show her the camping spot where he'd found the backpack, so for now she felt it best not to push. Just before dusk the evening before, Billy had come in the back door of the Blue Spot Café with the pack over one shoulder. Visiting the café was pretty much part of his routine: he often came in after the supper crowd had gone, to cadge leftover fries, and the owner usually obliged. Normally, the backpack would not have raised eyebrows, except that Sharnell had been asking questions on Main Street much of the day yesterday. The police down in Missoula had asked her to look around for a couple who'd been camping in the Schomberg area and were overdue on their return. Sharnell had talked to the town's eateries and outfitters, as well as several other likely stores.

They were three minutes or so along the logging road now. It ran straight, but the surface was rough, and Billy had a hard time maintaining his rigid pose.

"Up there," he said, suddenly pushing his hand in front of Sharnell's face to point out her side window. "Smelled smoke down here 'n' went up t'see. 'S'about coupla hunnert yards or so. Fools!"

Before he got into the car, Billy had told Sharnell he'd found the pack left behind at a campsite. During the telling he'd become quite upset over the fact that the campers had left the site without putting out their fire completely.

When the two of them reached the camping spot, it appeared much as Billy had said. The remains of a campfire were strewn in front of flattened grass where a tent had been pitched. Sharnell had to get to her knees to see them, but it didn't take her long to find the holes the tent pegs had made. She focused the camera she'd brought with her, and began to shoot the scene from various angles. Just like fiddling with the sun visor and the radio, taking pictures gave her something to do while she worked out her strategy. Clearly, she was going to have to challenge Billy with the flaw in his explanation of how he found the backpack. As well, she was going to have to have the campsite examined more thoroughly, and then she'd have to organize a search party. All that had to be arranged from town, however. For now, she felt it best to take Billy back to Schomberg before confronting him.

What is the flaw in Billy's explanation of how he found the backpack?

— 10 —

THE IDENTIKIT DECISION

The watch commander in charge of the unit covering a
rundown part of the city known as The Meadow was
Wally Bricken. An aging, overweight, desk-bound cop,
Wally, in his long years on the job, had developed a thick
skin of cynicism, not only out of disappointment in his fellow human beings and their capacity for evil, but also
because of a deep-seated disillusionment with the will of
his superiors to respond to it. This attitude accounted for
his look of surprise when he joined the meeting—already
in progress—up in Homicide on the third floor.

"This'll be one a' yer quick-'n'-dirtys," he'd told the desk
sergeant as he left his office. "Th' vic was just some hooker from over in Th' Meadow. Way I hear, she was cut up
pretty bad, but then . . ."

But for "just some hooker," Captain Spate of Homicide
seemed to have pulled out all the stops. While making the
few steps from her office door to his accustomed corner
chair for meetings like these, Wally was impressed by the
presence of two crime scene investigators, the head of Vice
and a sergeant from Robbery, one of the young computer
wizards from the lab—he didn't know the guy's name—
four homicide detectives, and a captain from highway
patrol! One of the CSI types was just finishing up.

" . . . So we think it's pretty clear this was a crime with
intent, not some spontaneous argument over money or
drugs. And not a crime of passion either: he cut her up in
the back seat of that car like he was taking a puzzle apart.
Whoever did this set out to kill somebody." He held up a

plastic evidence bag with a brown flask inside. "There are prints on this liquor bottle, but only hers are clear. The others are too smudged. A tiny trace of some kind of adhesive on the rim here. And this is weird. See this?" He pointed to a small, irregularly shaped blob stuck to the label.

"Looks like a booger!" someone blurted out.

Everyone chuckled except the crime scene investigator, who carried on without responding. "We're getting it analyzed. Now on the prints. Only her prints on the inside of the car—stolen car, of course. Seems kind of odd he'd be wearing gloves when he picked her up, because that could tip her off something's not right, but then with AIDS these days who knows? Anyway, we'll have more on the car by this afternoon; pathology report by then, too. Meantime . . . "

"Excuse me, Gerry," Captain Spate interrupted. "Now that Watch Commander Bricken has honored this task force with his presence—so nice of you to take the time, Wally—I think we should deal with the street canvass. That's got to get underway fast."

She continued before Wally could respond. "I don't think everyone here knows Arnold Sheen-Revy." She waved expansively at the young computer tech. "Go ahead, Arnold."

The young man reached behind him and brought out a picture on fluted white cardboard. "I have two dozen of these for you, Watch Commander," he said, holding up a computer-generated picture of the face of a male in his thirties.

One of the homicide detectives, an older one, spoke directly to Wally. "Two girls on the street think they saw the guy. Said he was cruising and came down the street twice, and you know how this kind of woman peers into cars a little more carefully than others do."

"This representation of the face is what they seem to agree on," the technician broke in. "Couldn't see eye color, of course, since it was after dark, but they both described the hair style and the moustache in the same way. Nothing remarkable about either one, unfortunately."

Wally started to speak, grateful that the captain's barb had seemed to disappear in the urgency of the situation, but she interrupted again.

"Right away, Wally—if you can manage that concept—I want you to get a copy of this picture into the hands of every street officer in your watch and do a blitz. Somebody in The Meadow has to have seen this guy, and the longer we wait the weaker their memories will be."

Wally looked directly at the young computer tech, pointedly ignoring Captain Spate. "These computer Identikits—they're easier than the old flip charts, aren't they? So how fast can you get me some copies without the moustache?" he asked.

"Without the moustache? Why do you want . . . oh, because he might shave it off?"

"No," Wally replied, "Because I'd say you've got evidence here that suggests it was a fake in the first place."

What evidence suggests to Wally that the moustache was a fake?

WAITING FOR SAHDEEN

Harry was slouched way down in the seat. The position enabled him to watch the street behind him in the side mirror and, at the same time, through the windshield he could keep an eye on the exit from the parking garage at Old Church Towers. An added bonus was that the position was reasonably comfortable. In the grubby old van they were using today, there weren't many comfortable positions. Beside him, Max had pulled his elbow back inside after a jogger had bumped it dodging through the sidewalk traffic. Max was sitting now with his chin balanced on top of the steering wheel, both arms hanging simian-like to the floor. The pair had been parked here on Dacey Street since two in the morning and still had a couple of hours to go before their relief showed up.

Harry focused on the mirror, where another clutch of cyclists was beginning to fill the frame. There were about a dozen in this bunch, the third in the past few minutes. He watched them top the slight rise and then gain speed on the down-grade. At dawn, when the motor traffic was lighter, Harry had rather enjoyed listening to the tires sing as the bikes swished past. He'd even worked out a counting system, placing every cyclist in one of three different sound categories.

"You do that kind of thing when you're on a stakeout," he explained to Max, who was at it for the first time. Max just grunted. He declined to participate.

Traffic was thicker now, and the city noises, too, so Harry had abandoned the tire-song count. Dacey Street was a straight run to Oliver Mowat Park, so even though it was a weekend, the cars and bikes and joggers and delivery vans made it just like any other day. Harry still looked for things to keep him awake, however, for it didn't seem like Sahdeen was going to show. That's if he was even up there in Old Church Towers like the tip said. As far as Harry was concerned, Sahdeen was long gone. He knew the city well, and he knew how to keep a low profile and disappear.

Yet another stream of bicycles showed up in the mirror. And behind them a pair of vintage cars. "You know what I'd do, Max, if I was a terrorist like Sahdeen?" Harry said. "Instead of wasting all my time with bombs and threats and that, what I'd do if I wanted to really disrupt North American culture is I'd figure out a way to make all the Spandex in the country come apart at once. On a Sunday morning."

Max grunted, and Harry kept on: "And then what I'd do, I'd—"

"Gray Ford Windstar!" Max broke in. His chin had come off the steering wheel and he was focused on the exit of Old Church Towers where a Windstar with signal flashing was waiting to turn onto Dacey Street. "Piled up with junk, right? Like a family going to the beach? Isn't that what the tip said?" Max sat up even straighter and turned on the ignition. "That's Sahdeen! Gotta be!"

Both men waited for the Windstar to turn onto Dacey, and when it did Harry reached over and turned the key to Off. "Not Sahdeen," he said, slouching back down in the seat. "Get the plate number when it comes closer and call it in just in case it's a decoy, but that's not Sahdeen. He wouldn't be that stupid."

What did the van driver do that was so stupid?

— 12 —
JUST A DEAD BATTERY

When the car didn't start, Lily diSantos could have simply chosen to get out, walk about ten steps back to the garage, and holler to one of the mechanics to bring booster cables. Instead, she first walked about ten steps in the opposite direction, to the little booth that housed the precinct's equipment records. She wanted to know who had used the patrol car last and parked it with the door not closed properly and the onboard computer left on so the battery had drained.

It came as no surprise to Lily, and even with a bit of satisfaction, when she discovered the culprit was O'Quinn. His demerit sheet already looked like a kindergarten birthday card. What did lift Lily's eyebrows was a touch of coincidence. O'Quinn had checked the patrol car back in at 4:00 A.M. this morning, when his shift ended. He and his partner, a rookie named Scrotin, had been on perimeter duty at the Eckman robbery for about two hours, right from the time it was called in. It was the Eckman robbery that had forced Lily out of her office this morning and into the parking lot, where it just happened that the only available car wouldn't start.

Normally, Lily diSantos did not go to the site of a robbery, even when pressure came down from above—as it most certainly had in this case. Sometime after midnight last night, the Queen Margaret Necklace had taken wing from its accustomed resting place in Abraham Eckman's wall safe, and by dawn this morning the president of the company that insured it had called the mayor, who called the commissioner, who called the chief, and so on down the pipe.

Even so, Lily might have stuck to her desk, where the week's paperwork was already spilling over the sides. She had already sent the head of Robbery to run the pair of detectives on the case.

What had pulled her into the situation directly was a development with possible diplomatic complications, raising the case to more than a straightforward heist. At first light this morning, a neighbor of the Eckmans walking his dog had found a small jeweler's case and a piece of paper in the alley behind the row of wealthy homes where the Eckman mansion held prominence.

"Not the kind of thing one usually pays attention to," the neighbor had explained, "but with all those flashing red lights on the street in the middle of the night, well . . . "

The jeweler's case was empty; it was the paper that drew interest. It had a rather crudely drawn layout of the Eckmans' main floor and a short notation in Arabic. Beneath that was what looked like the beginnings of a symbol, as though the artist had started drawing it and then had changed his mind.

Before leaving headquarters Lily had withdrawn the note from the evidence locker. She was staring at it now, lying on the passenger seat. She had finally gotten around to calling a mechanic, and was waiting for him to pull another vehicle closer to complete the battery boost. The paper was a sheet of expensive hotel stationery, and was so clean and creamy that the writing on it almost seemed a violation. When it was first shown to her, Lily had noted immediately that it was from a hotel favored by diplomats from the Middle

East, and, although she'd resisted the thought, this made the partly finished symbol look very much like one used by the Hezbollah. It didn't help that the Eckmans were well-known supporters of Israeli territorial expansion.

"Captain diSantos? You ready?" The mechanic snapped Lily back to the present. "Just turn the key. She should start."

The car did just that, roaring to life with a bit more noise than Lily intended, for she'd pressed the accelerator hard. She reached above her and turned the interior light switch from Door to On and back again, then turned off the slapping windshield wipers. Instinctively, she turned off the computer when it began to beep, and then swore softly as she realized she needed to have it on. Under her breath, she swore at O'Quinn, too, for his carelessness.

"Anything else, Captain? You were right. Just a dead battery." The mechanic had closed the hood and was leaning into the windshield. He had to shout because Lily still had the accelerator down—something she vaguely remembered her first husband telling her to do after a boost.

"You don't need to run 'er quite so hard, Captain. She's ready to go now." A touch embarrassed, Lily gave him a nonchalant salute and pulled out of the lot as quickly as her dignity would permit. It didn't take more than a few seconds for the embarrassment to wear off, however, especially when Lily suddenly connected the dots and realized the diplomatic issue was most likely a setup, a distraction from a good old-fashioned jewelry heist.

What leads Lily diSantos to the idea that the diplomatic issue is probably a distraction?

AN EXCERPT FROM SCENE THREE

Fogarty and Curtis sit at a desk center stage. Fogarty is in uniform behind the desk. Curtis sits backwards on a wooden chair in front. A spot lights them; the rest of the stage is in darkness.

FOGARTY: My problem is, I'm holding three suspects downstairs, and there was only one shooter, so I gotta let two of 'em go. Question is which one to keep?

CURTIS: Maybe you should ...no ... Run it by me one more time.

FOGARTY: Sure. Victim is Joseph Beingessner, fifty-eight. Shot in his bed at about 1:15 A.M ... well, not "about," at 1:15 A.M. Last house on the north road out a' town. Pitch-black night, no moon or stars and the nearest streetlight is out. Him and the wife are in bed asleep. Real stifler last night—you know that—so they've got a ceiling fan going and a fan beside the bed. The shooter gets into their bedroom and puts three shots into Joe. Uses an old Smith and Wesson .38, so it's one shot at a time. Fast enough, but none of your automatic poppatta-pop. The fourth shot goes into the wife's leg. She says she woke up with the first shot—so she thinks—but it takes her a couple of seconds to react. Reasonable enough, I'd say. Then she screams and kicks the sheet off. That's when the bullet hits her. 'Sa double bed, see? Looks like the shot was meant for Beingessner, but she got in the way.

Anyway, then the shooter hustles out over this little balcony off their bedroom. Just a small drop, one story, and the ravine's right there. We're not sure yet if he got in that way. By the balcony, I mean. The problem is, we got a wit-ness—or a survivor. Don't know what to call her yet, but either way the wife doesn't see anything, not even a body shape 'cause it's so dark. And she can't get the bed lamp to work because it's unplugged for the fan! They left the clock plugged in.

CURTIS: Seems you worked pretty fast considering there's so little evidence. Three suspects? And it's barely twelve hours ago?

FOGARTY: Found the Smith and Wesson at first light down in the ravine. No prints—what else is new?—but it looks like the shooter dropped it. Didn't intend to, but maybe because he was running . . . It's dark in that ravine and full of brush. Anyway, the gun belongs to the guy that lives in their base-ment. The Beingessners rent out this self-contained apart-ment. Separate entrance and all that. We picked him up first.

CURTIS: Alibi?

FOGARTY: Nothing that would impress a jury. Says he went to a late movie over in Silver Creek. Got out about twenty after midnight—he's got the time right, but any idiot can fig-ure that—and then he says he had a flat out on Horseshoe Road. That checks out pretty much, too, with the tracks and the gravel all stirred up, but he could have done it all in advance. Then he says he came home about two to find us all over the place.

CURTIS: This guy have a motive?

FOGARTY: Not like the other two. I mean, the whole town hates Beingessner. He's screwed everybody at one time or another, but this guy . . . he's hardly been around long enough.

CURTIS: Maybe he and Mrs. Beingessner were . . .

FOGARTY: I'd be some surprised. I've known Liddie for . . . heck, we went to school together. She's just not the type. 'Sides, I'm pretty sure this guy goes the other way, if you know what I mean.

CURTIS: So why are you still holding him?

FOGARTY: Well . . . it is his gun. And he's a bit of a drifter, a loner. But then, so's Beingessner's own kid!

CURTIS: Yes, that son of theirs you have in custody . . . he their only child?

FOGARTY: No, there's two more boys. All three of them took off as soon as they were grown enough. The other two are out in Alberta. Riggers. RCMP confirmed them a couple hours ago. Roly, the one I've got downstairs? He's the youngest. Left home about a year ago. Do I remember that night! Him and Joe had a knock-down-drag-out right on the main street! Yet he came back about six months later. Lives in Silver Creek now. And before you ask, his alibi's about the same as the tenant, the gun owner. For that matter, "Hep" Scharnhorst's alibi is even weaker.

CURTIS: Scharnhorst . . . number three. He's the one that's feuded with Beingessner for some thirty years or more, right? Both of them in the same business, but Beingessner wins out, almost puts Scharnhorst under, so that he's barely scratching by now. And you told me something about Scharnhorst and Lid . . . Mrs. Beingessner . . .

FOGARTY: Both of them were hard after Liddie, right from high school. We all thought she was going to marry Hep. Sure looked like it. Then all of a sudden she ups and marries Joe. It just crushed him. Hep, I mean.

CURTIS: And he never married. Lives alone, so naturally

there's nobody to confirm that he was asleep in bed at 1:15 A.M. last night, as he says.

FOGARTY: You can see my problem, can't you? I sure hated bringing him in. And the other two, for that matter.

CURTIS: Still, if you look at the crime scene, only one of the three is a prime suspect.

FOGARTY: Really? Which one?

Which one is a prime suspect, and on what basis does Curtis make that claim?

— 14 —

THE NEW DEPUTY
TAKES A WRONG STEP

"Now take a look around. You can see for yourself these cows got plenty a' good pasture. The rain we had last week and a coupla days ago, a shower again last night—why, the grass is growin' real good."

Tim looked around dutifully and nodded. He didn't have the foggiest idea what constituted good pasture or bad, and he wasn't about to risk a discussion of the topic with Carter Spence.

"And water. They always got plenty a' water. Down there in the trough at the far corner. Comes in gravity-fed from the creek, so it's fresh all the time. No need for my cows to be crossin' into no neighbor's field to graze. They got plenty right here. Don't know what goes around in that Joe Schenk's head sometimes, him sayin' it was my cows got into his turnips last night. Bet you any money it was his own cattle what done it!"

Before calling on Carter Spence, Tim had spent some time at Joe Schenk's, so he had a pretty good idea what a field of turnips looked like, even though Joe's field, the one next to where he was now standing, had been pretty badly trampled. According to Joe, Carter Spence's cattle had broken out of their own field last night, jumped the shallow ditch that ran along the property line between the two farms, and feasted on his yet-to-be-harvested turnips.

Carter was still going. "Now the ditch here along the field 'tween me and Joe's? Not a big one, mind you. You can see that. We put 'er in some years back for drainage. Now most times you can contain a herd with something that simple, 'specially if they got plenty to eat here, like mine do. But not me! I go the next step. Electric fence. You know what they say about good fences and good neighbors."

Tim had speculated that the single strand of wire running the length of the field on Carter's side of the ditch was an electrified fence. The wire was strung from plastic insulators attached to thin, evenly spaced metal posts. He could see that Carter's cows had grazed up to a respectful distance from the wire, but under it and around the posts, the grass was high. At several points, grass and weeds hid the wire completely.

"Now I want you to see for yourself this here's a workin' fence." Carter motioned at Tim to follow. "Some fellas, they don't . . . Careful you don't step in . . . ! Oh, that's too bad. Fresh one, too. I got an old shirt in the truck, you can clean up with."

While Carter went on about the merits of electric fencing, Tim followed along with one eye on his right shoe, in his mind replaying the mental tape that reminded him why he'd left homicide in Detroit to become a deputy in rural Lambton County.

"Just step over the fence." Carter's voice came back into Tim's consciousness. "Careful, now! I keep the wire low—cows're more sensitive at the knees. Still, don't want you to get a jolt, though. Now, just come over here to the box—the transformer. Listen. See? I got 'er set at three. Meaning she sends out a charge every three seconds."

In precisely that time sequence, Tim could hear a distinct clunk emanating from the metal box that held the transformer. He nodded at Carter Spence, indicating his agreement that, yes, the equipment was turned on. Then, for the first time since coming into the field, he spoke out loud. "But there's no charge going down the wire, is there, Mr. Spence?"

How does Tim know the electrified fence system is not working properly?

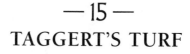

— 15 —
TAGGERT'S TURF

P.C. Simpson Taggert was the oldest beat cop on the force. He may well have been the oldest beat cop in the entire country, but that didn't bother him in the least, for his life as a cop was just the way he wanted it. For Simpson Taggert, there were no politics; there was no sucking up to the brass, no pressure to fatten his personnel file. Best of all, he had his own turf. Sure, other cops took shifts on the same beat, for he couldn't be on duty twenty-four hours a day. But the others came and went. He stayed.

A few seconds ago, as he turned south off Prince Boulevard heading down Fawcett to number 41, Taggert had allowed himself a short, uncharacteristic smile when he realized that today was an anniversary—one that only he would remember, but that was just fine with him. Thirty-five years ago today, June 19, he'd turned down a promotion. There had been two more offers after that, both declined, and then they stopped. But with each offer he'd extracted a promise.

Taggert interrupted his reverie to pull over to the curb so he could look at the flowers in front of number 20. In many ways, Fawcett Avenue, like a lot of the residential streets around here, was a beat cop's dream. Quiet. Good people. Not big houses, but really well cared for. The lots were too small for professional landscaping, but every frontyard had flowerbeds, and every backyard had a large, mature maple or elm, sometimes two or three. Number 20 he'd always called the "begonia house," for year after year the owners planted dark-leafed, red fibrous begonias. A bit boring to some, perhaps, but Taggert had learned enough from his wife to respect their choice.

"Morning sun for fibrous begonias," MaryKate would chant, "shade for your tuberous ones, and afternoon sun for your daisies." And he and MaryKate had planted that way every spring until the cancer took her.

It was because of MaryKate that he'd said no to the vice squad thirty-five years ago. They'd just bought a little house not unlike number 20, a fixer-upper that they wanted to work on together. Taggert was a good cop, and it wasn't hard to get the brass to agree to leaving him on the beat—his beat—the one he liked and came to know so well.

He pulled away from the curb before he started attracting attention. No use upsetting anyone at the start of the day with the sight of a police car in front of their house. For the same reason he didn't stop at 41, just slowed enough to confirm the details in his memory bank: short sidewalk bisecting the small lot and running up to wide, wooden steps that led in turn to an old-fashioned verandah. Both sides of the steps were crowded by a pair of overgrown yews, with nicely maintained beds of periwinkle leading away to short cedar hedges that marked the limits of the property.

Taggert had been inside the house a few years before. Not a big deal. The husband, Trevor Banjee, was a pretty heavy drinker and had gotten drunk enough to frighten his wife into calling the station. By the time Taggert was able to respond, Banjee had passed out. He'd meant to come back the next day and read the riot act, but never got around to it. And Taggert had been there again only a month ago, just before he left on vacation. Part of a wider situation this time, a peeping Tom.

There had been quite a number of 9-1-1 calls, several from Mrs. Banjee.

Fawcett ended in a cul-de-sac and Taggert made a U-turn to go back to Prince Boulevard. He didn't even glance at the "begonia house" this time. When he was upset, Taggert paid far less attention to his favorite spots, and he was particularly upset now. That young snippet at the coroner's office— she'd have to be told a thing or two about how to do proper investigations on his turf. Last week, the final week of Taggert's vacation, Mrs. Banjee had killed her husband, and that young whatever-her-name-was—he'd only met her once—had ruled it involuntary manslaughter.

At a red light, Taggert took the summary sheet from the file on the seat beside him.

"A beautiful sunny morning," it quoted Mrs. Banjee,

I was out before the heat came. Trevor was still in bed— that's what I thought anyway; he usually is these days. And I was bent over, working on my ground-cover beds, my periwinkle, with the hand cultivator. Facing away from the street. And all of a sudden there was this shadow of someone right over me. So I swung! I mean, I was really scared! You know with that prowler around now, and it's always at dawn that he comes! Those prongs on the cultivator? They hit Trevor right on the side of the head, and he . . . [Subject too distraught to continue.]

Further along Prince Boulevard, Simpson Taggert turned into a Drive-Thru. He was hearing MaryKate again.

"Never hurts to stop and have a cup of coffee before you jump into something. In the time it takes for the coffee to cool, you might just change your mind."

What Taggert thought the time might do was calm him down enough to approach the young woman at the coroner's office directly rather than go over her head. She was dead wrong—about the involuntary part, anyway—but then, as MaryKate would certainly have pointed out, he was young once, too, and made mistakes. Besides, he thought, it's probably better to have her onside if she's going to be working on Taggert's turf.

Why does Simpson Taggert disagree with the "involuntary" element in the killing of Mr. Banjee?

— 16 —
I SAW HIM DO IT!

Director's notes to camera crew:

This scene will run behind the end of the opening credits so we will need very sharp images.

#1. Medium Distance
Camera takes in all of the small white frame house and the backyard as far as the woodpile. Set angle so that the back half of the house on the other side can be seen, too. Be certain the green exterior trim on this next house and the green shutters on the kitchen window are clearly seen, so that when the young woman is killed in [# 5] there is no doubt that this is the house where the murder happens. HOLD THIS SAME CAMERA DISTANCE AND ANGLE UNTIL THE OLD WOMAN REACHES THE FRONT OF THE WOODPILE.

Old woman appears at left from behind the woodpile. Walks through the snow around to front of the woodpile. Despite her age, she's spry, but walks slightly bent. Wears an old dress and an apron, a kerchief tied tightly around her chin, and a heavy man's jacket. Thick winter boots. Important that we can see her breath to indicate it's very cold. She carries a wicker basket. Camera does not move until woman gets to front of woodpile.

#2. Medium Close
Then move in slowly to medium close. Need to be in close enough to see she is definitely a senior. Gray hair, wire-rimmed glasses, etc. [NOTE TO KELLY: we will

shoot this 3–4 times. I want to stay back as far as possible from the woman, but we have to see her age. It's a big issue later in the courtroom scenes.]

Use minimum camera movement for the next small bit of action. She sets the basket on the woodpile. [KELLY: the basket has eggs in it. Try to get this without being obvious.] Stoops to gather a few thin pieces of wood, stops, and then with both hands takes her glasses off briefly to rub one eye as if there might be dirt in it. Puts wood under one arm, picks up the basket with the other and

#3. Medium Distance and Dolly In

moves to the back door of the white frame-house. Follow woman to the house. Dolly in as she approaches the back door. Keep moving in so that, as she opens the door, the camera becomes her eyes. We now see only what she sees.

#4. Medium Close, Slow Pan Left

Follow her eyes from the wood-burning stove in the kitchen across the sink with its hand pump. There are two oil lamps on the counter to the left of the sink. Do not linger on these, BUT pan slowly enough to make sure they're noted. Pan stops at a window that looks across to the house with the green trim. THIS SHOT SHOULD NOT BE LONGER THAN 5–6 SECONDS.

#5. Medium Distance

Center on the rear window of the house with green trim. The victim is just inside and is clearly visible. [KELLY: we'll be shooting this at least twice, once with her wearing a blonde wig, and another time with a red one. We'll check the rushes to see which is most visible.] Hold the distance while the man chokes her, then

#6. Short Quick Zoom

do this one handheld, so we get impression the old woman moves closer to her own window. Two-second hold on the man who has done the killing. All we see is his right side from hips up, then

#7. Rapid Pan Left

to old-fashioned wall telephone. [KELLY: shoot this with a short zoom in to the telephone, and also without a zoom, and hold on the telephone after the pan. We'll decide later.]

End of Scene

Get some extra shots outside, the woodpile, the houses, etc., without any of the actors in them. Couple of the snow, too, with some different angles.

Marcel, I think there's something wrong here. I don't think the woman would be able to see the killing. In fact I think the whole thing is wrong.

Kelly

Why does Kelly think the old woman will not be able to see the killing, and that, in fact, "the whole thing is wrong"?

— 17 —

A LOGICAL SUSPECT

Her supervisor had warned there would be tears, but parole officers, even the softer ones like Megan, were used to them. Real tears, alligator tears, tears of frustration, cries of anger or disbelief, the soft flow that comes with acceptance and defeat—they were all variations on a theme that played like Muzak throughout a parole officer's day. Yet tears seemed out of place in the big commercial greenhouse where Megan was now standing. It was so full of life and beauty and promise. Behind Sonja Lopash, the woman doing the crying, hundreds—no thousands—of daisies stood erect and proud in precise rows, their white petals gleaming. Behind Megan, stretching back to the door through which she'd come in, banks of pert yellow marigolds stood at attention on one side of the long aisle, confidently saluting the mass of red salvia on the other.

The place was simply bursting with growth and, to Megan, seemed like an encouraging, reassuring environment to work in. Definitely not a place for tears.

"He was here when it happened, Normie was!" Sonja insisted between sniffles. "He had to be. You can see for yourself!" Her runny nose disappeared for a few seconds behind a denim sleeve. The action triggered a sharp change of tone. "Y'know, you people have always picked on my brother. The police, too! Every single time something like this happens, you take him to jail before you even bother to look for anybody else!"

Although Megan knew how pointless it was to argue in a situation like this, she tried to explain anyway.

"The police are only doing what they have to, Mrs. Lopash. Normie was clearly identified by several people yesterday at the corner of Main and Seneca, and that—"

"There's a 7-11 there!" Sonja's anger flared dangerously. "Are you trying to tell me if you're on parole you can't go buy a pack of smokes?"

Megan kept her voice soft and deliberate. "There are many places to buy cigarettes, and that intersection is only a block from the little girl's school. You know as well as I do that a condition of Normie's parole is that he keep at least 500 yards away from any place where children gather."

"The children were inside their school!"

"Mrs. Lopash . . . may I call you Sonja? The problem is that only a few minutes later, many of them—including the missing girl—crossed Main and Seneca. It was just before lunchtime."

Megan did not add the information her supervisor had given her only an hour before. The police had taken Normie into custody this morning because a man answering his description had been seen talking to the missing girl yesterday afternoon. And later in the day, at dusk, she had been seen getting into a small green truck. Lopash Nurseries used small green trucks. On the other hand, this had happened at the other end of the city, and none of the witnesses was able to describe the driver of the truck because a city-wide power failure had taken out the street lighting a few minutes before. But all agreed it was a man.

"That gives probable cause, no question," the supervisor had said to Megan. "As soon as the confounded power comes back on, we'll get Normie's file from central records, and if the victims in his two previous convictions match this girl even a little, he's going back inside!"

Sonja's brief defiance didn't last long. Her spirit was too worn down by care and limited hope. "My brother, he's . . . he's . . . Well, okay, Normie's a little different, I'll grant you that. And, yes, there were those two times when . . . But he's had all that therapy at the jail—the hospital, I mean. He's better now. Such a good worker, too. Even my husband . . .

"Do you know my husband didn't want him here? We had the worst row when Normie came to live with us. But now we could hardly get on without him. See, we're all automated now. These plants in here, every day they're watered automatically at sunset. The fertilizing is all computerized; we even adjust the amount of light. But you still have all kinds of donkey work that machines and computers can't do. Some of it's pretty dirty, and Normie, he . . . well, he doesn't complain. And when it's necessary to do the more complicated stuff? Like start the backup generator, drive the forklift or the trucks, test the pH levels? He can do that, too! He's the only one besides us who can do what needs doing around here!"

Megan turned toward the salvia so she wouldn't have to look Sonja in the eye. "The best thing for Normie right now," she said over her shoulder, "would be if you and your husband, and maybe one or two other people, could say he was right here with you last night when the little girl got into that truck."

Sonja's voice was barely a whisper. She shook her head, although Megan was still focused on the red flowers to her left. "Alone," she said. "He was here all alone. Normie was looking after . . . My husband and I . . . It's the first time in months we took a couple of days for ourselves. We came right back when we heard about the power failure. Drove all night . . . but he was here! Normie was here! He had to be! Don't you see?"

Megan's professional training had taught her never to commit herself, but as she turned back toward Sonja, she nodded vigorously in spite of it. "I agree, Sonja," she said. "I agree."

What evidence has convinced Megan that "Normie was here"?

— 18 —

TIVERTON VS. CAPELLI

It was unusually cool for the last week of July, so when she got out of the car Leona had pulled a nylon shell over her t-shirt. She took it off when she reached the accident site. Trekking along the narrow dirt road at the edge of the park had warmed her up, and now that she was surrounded by thick stands of maple and oak the chilly wind no longer had an effect.

Sitting on the exposed root of a giant maple, she could look down into the gully where, nine months before, Tiverton had run into the strand of wire Capelli had put up. It was a shallow depression, the gully, just as Capelli said it was, and almost perfectly round, not unlike a soup bowl. It wasn't very large: Leona judged it to be about the size of two, maybe three tennis courts. The narrow track running down the sides and along the bottom, the one the mountain bikers used, was beginning to grow in again, returning to its natural state. Tiverton had probably been the last one to use it because of the publicity surrounding his injury.

Leona studied the wire strung across the path about mid-calf high on the park side of the gully floor. One end of the wire was stapled to a young oak tree. The other was wound around a ... she didn't know much about wild shrubs but, whatever it was, it wasn't going to be torn loose by a mountain bike. Obviously, the wire was meant to be more than a token. And it was clearly visible, even from a distance. Furthermore, Capelli said he'd hung orange marker ribbons from it, and there they were, making the wire even more obvious . . . one, two . . . altogether she could count six of them.

She felt just a bit guilty that this was the first time she'd been to the site, what with the hearing only two days away. It was going to be a sticky, unpleasant case. Tiverton, who was suing Capelli, had the advantage of sympathy on his side. He was only twenty-three and was now looking forward to spending the rest of his life in a wheelchair. His version of events was that he'd been following a path regularly used by mountain bikers, and at high speed had been tripped by a hidden wire. Capelli maintained that he was simply trying to stop mountain bikers from trespassing on his land and causing destruction, and that, yes, he had put up a wire, as any landowner was allowed to do, but he'd marked it clearly with ribbons.

The bike path ran along the road where Leona had walked in. At the point where the road petered out, the path veered sharply to the right into a national park. But bikers, as they are known to do, had begun creating their own trail, and over time had created a loop into Capelli's gully. Instead of turning right into the park, what they did was turn left through some trees to make a sharp drop into the gully. Then, by pedaling hard across the bottom, they would shoot up the other side, do a one-eighty around some more trees, retrace the run, and only then go into the park.

As often happened in litigation of this type, each side had strong and weak points to its case. When she'd reluctantly agreed to take on Capelli—he'd approached her by saying he needed a "damn lawyer"—Leona's first instinct was to settle out of court. There was just too much gray in the case. Ribbons might or might not have been tied to the wire at the time Tiverton was injured; it was his word against Capelli's. No Trespassing signs were an issue: some case law suggested they were necessary, but other judgements said they were not. Capelli didn't have any. There was also an ethical call: if bikers had been crossing Capelli's gully for some time, was it his responsibility to warn them that he was going to close it? Still another point was the placement of the wire. Tiverton's attorney had already argued that the wire should have been strung at the top edge of the gully. But Capelli's property line was at the bottom, and that was precisely where he'd put the wire.

Leona sighed and drew the nylon shell over her head once more. Too bad it's such a cool day, she thought. This would be a nice place to relax. The gully—it really did look like a soup bowl!—had so many big trees around it: oak and beech, a lot of maple. Too bad the sun was hiding. The birds, too. She got to her feet.

"A good move, my coming here," she said out loud. "There's no way Tiverton could have seen that wire. If Capelli's smart, he'll listen to me and settle."

Why does Leona believe there is "no way Tiverton could have seen that wire"?

— 19 —

TREVOR WILKEY'S JOURNAL

17 November, 1921

To: Sir Reynulf Playfair, K.G., Lieutenant-Governor,
    Transjordan Protectorate

From: Major Byron Gordon, Qazar el Azraq Garrison

Sir,

Further to my report of 30 August 1921, which noted the unexpected return of Lieutenant Neville Eby from the expedition to Wadi al Mira, I regret to inform you that the remains of Captain Trevor Wilkey were found by Bedouin tribesmen in the Syrian Desert. I conclude from their description, and from details in Captain Wilkey's journal, that his death was the result of dehydration and exposure. News of the discovery and his personal effects were delivered here to the garrison on the 15th inst.

I have ordered Lieutenant Eby confined to barracks pending your recommendation concerning charges against him in this case. The following entries from Captain Wilkey's journal explain my action:

31 May 1921: Qazar el Azraq: Much excitement today, for we will leave tomorrow as scheduled. What true adventure! When we reach Wadi al Mira, we will be the first Europeans ever to have crossed this part of the Syrian Desert! No maps, of course, but we know the general direction, and we have our trusty sextant and compass. Last of the native drivers hired, and three extra camels purchased. Neville excited, too. Seems to have forgotten our rivalry over Margaret. Good thing! Major Gordon had all three of us to the mess tonight for a farewell dinner.

1 June: Under way! Not much distance today, but Qazar el Azraq now off the horizon. Usual first day shakeout. Extra camels a wise decision. Had to turn one loose today: completely uncontrollable. Drivers in good spirit.

10 June: Twenty miles! Won't do this well every day, but at this rate will make Wadi Osr in ten days or less. Gave up another camel. Irascible beasts at any time, but ours do not seem well broken. Neville far ahead, so I had to deal with things. Got a rather sharp kick for my trouble. Drivers found that humorous. (I didn't.)

18 June: Wadi Osr: Making excellent time. Camels more manageable now with routine and hard work. Yesterday uneventful. Reached Wadi Osr an hour before dusk.

21 June: Possible problem. If I can believe our head-man, Ahmed, it seems the drivers were not aware our goal is Wadi al Mira. Their dialect difficult, but I can make out "insane British" easily enough. Situation resolved by offering more money. A camel gone during the night, a driver, too. Impossible to ignore the 2 + 2 of that.

24 June: Good distance despite heat. Terrain much rougher now. Neville leading, as usual. Just as well, since I'm better with the squabbles. Our drivers don't much like one another. One more disappeared last night, but didn't take a camel. Neville had quite an argument with Ahmed, who says the stars show we are too far west. Had to intervene to put Ahmed in his place.

27 June: Heat unbelievable despite semi-mountainous

terrain. Ahmed says we must now begin travel well before dawn and rest in late afternoon. Neville agrees. Heat is affecting him more than me. I agreed as much to soothe Ahmed as anything else. He distrusts me. Still making good time. Wadi Osr a distant memory now.

1 July: Disaster! Neville has taken a bad tumble. Out front as usual. We came upon him unconscious over the lip of a crevasse. Awoke an hour or so later, but he is acting odd. Not sure he's over it. No broken bones, thank heaven. Worst of all: sextant went down the crevasse! No hope of recovery. Fortunately, Neville had the compass in his pocket.

2 July: Rested all day. Neville better but still uncertain. Passed out twice, but briefly. Worst problem is, Ahmed and two remaining drivers want to turn back. Money does not appeal any more. Threats did the job for now.

3 July: Under way again. Neville not strong. Only five miles today because of balky camel and Neville's condition.

4 July: Crisis! Neville must turn back. Can't stay awake. Disoriented. He feels I should come, too, but that is no way to complete our task, and he knows it. Ahmed will go with him, which he is happy to do. The compass will stay with me. Fortunately, Neville made the final plotting for Wadi al Mira and set the compass while we still had the sextant. I still have the two drivers and the best of the camels will go with me. Neville will take lion's share of the water to see them back to Wadi Osr. I estimate al Mira in less than a week, so shouldn't need much.

5 July: Said our farewells before dawn. Good progress

today, but terrain is far rougher than we were warned. I have a bad feeling about the drivers.

8 July: Drivers gone this morning, but in the Bedouin way they left me a share of water! Perhaps their leaving is for the best, as I made more distance today than any day yet. Wadi al Mira should be close.

12 July: Heat is unbearable. Full moon tomorrow, so I will travel at night as much as possible. By my original estimates, should certainly have reached Wadi al Mira by now. Probably tomorrow. Terrain getting much more difficult.

15 July: Water almost gone. Must make al Mira or find water soon.

? July: No water. Outlook poor. Tell Margaret she is ever in my thoughts.

Sir, as you can see, there is a specific reason to attribute blame to Lieutenant Eby in Captain Wilkey's death, and I await your orders in the matter.

Respectfully,
Byron Gordon, Maj.

What is the "specific reason" Major Gordon refers to?

20

NEXT DOOR TO THE CHIEF

Antonina "Tony" Morello was a good cop. She was the highest ranking woman in a department that had been notoriously slow to accept the idea of gender equality, and her promotions had come about solely as a result of excellent performance. That was one reason Tony took such particular interest in the professional behavior of young female recruits. Her interest, however, did not always manifest in a gentle, motherly style, as Officer Cadet Rena Fineberg was discovering.

"No, Cadet Fineberg," Tony's words came spitting out. "It is not cool that we are in the house next door to the police chief! It is interesting, perhaps even intriguing, certainly unusual, but it is not cool! Furthermore, three months from now, when you graduate from the police academy—if you graduate—nothing will ever be cool again while you have that uniform on! Except the weather. And your temper!"

Her voice dropped suddenly in force and volume as she recognized the irony of her last comment. "Look, kid. It's just that when you're a cop, you're different from everybody else, and that difference is part of your power. So don't lose it by talking sloppy. 'Cool' is sloppy!"

The cadet still had such a look of fright on her face that Tony went further. "Relax. I've seen your reports from the academy; you're doing just fine." She used a tissue to wipe the perspiration from her forehead. "Of all the over-used words in your generation, that's the one I hate most. And with all this heat and humidity in front of the big storm we're supposed to get today, I guess I'm a bit cranky.

"Now . . . " Tony shifted to teacher mode. "You're right that this call to the chief's next-door neighbor is a bit out of the ordinary, and there's no question that there's politics in it. Technically—you must know this by now from the academy—it's a Six-Two-Two: Person Reported Missing. But Mr. Litt's been gone less than a day. He left the house at, what . . . " She looked at her watch. ". . . 9:30 this morning, and it's now just after 4:00 P.M. If anybody else called in with this, we'd give it at least till tomorrow morning, maybe even a bit more. But Litt's sister called the chief on his private number. What does that tell you?"

Cadet Fineberg, who had been standing rigid as a post, began to nod her head. "Means she . . . " The young woman stopped and cleared her throat. "It suggests they know each other quite well, and Chief Munson feels an obligation to her."

Tony almost interrupted to compliment Rena's new-found language skills, but instead waited for more.

Rena continued: "But the chief probably does not regard the situation as all that serious, which is why he asked you to send a cadet instead of diverting a regular patrol officer."

This time, Tony put out the compliment: "Good reasoning." She stepped over to one of the open windows, hoping in vain to feel a breeze. "You'd think he'd have air conditioning," she muttered to herself before adding, "and I am here to back you up—standard procedure—because your mentor officer had to go out on a Code Three. So," Tony wiped her forehead again, "now that I'm here, what else do we have?"

Grateful to be strictly business now, Rena Fineberg opened her notebook. "Mr. Litt left the house at 9:30 A.M. for a dentist appointment at 9:50. Just a regular checkup, and he left the dental office at about 10:20. I verified that—the dentist thing, I mean. According to his sister, he phoned from the parking lot to say he had just been to the dentist and was going to run a quick errand and then go home. The appointment had taken less time than he'd thought it would, so he asked her to pop over around 11:00 to continue an ongoing family discussion about investments. The sister phoned Chief Munson at 2:00 P.M."

Tony nodded. "Anything else?"

"Yeah. This is where it gets a bit funny. The wife—er— Mrs. Litt says he told her he'd be out all day with this and that. Didn't say just what. Might even miss dinner."

Tony frowned. Both women had been sitting in a room off the front entrance when she'd come in, but they did not appear to be enjoying conversation, much less each other's company. "And then what?" she asked Rena.

Rena swallowed noisily. "Then I figured there's something going on here, but, you know, the rules are cadets don't do interviews. By that time, I knew you were on your way over, so I asked if he had an office or den or something where I could wait."

"And that's when they ushered you into his office here?"

"Yeah—well, Mrs. Litt did. I could tell the sister didn't like the idea. Seems nobody's allowed in here but the mister himself." Rena's eyes widened suddenly and she spread both arms wide. "Isn't this some office? I mean, is this an organized person, or what? And this is where he works.

There's not a single piece of paper out of place!"

Tony had indeed noticed the precision of the office. Every book on every shelf stood in rigid order. The piles of paper beside his printer looked like members of a drill team at inspection time. What had struck her first when she entered was an easel board on one wall, where hand-written notes appeared in a small, deliberate, perfectly horizontal script. There were three separate columns. The tidy script beneath the heading "Complete" was blue; under "Current" it was yellow; and the "Projected" column was in red. Primary colors.

"And look at this!" Rena turned to a small black radio and turned up the volume button. "I turned it down when I came in. Don't like his music. Now watch!" She closed the door and a classical music station beamed into the room. She opened the door and it stopped. "Coo—, I mean, it's hooked up to a door-jamb switch! Is this a pro-grammed person, or what?"

"Yet he doesn't have air conditioning," Tony mused.

"Mrs. Litt says he's allergic. Here's something else. Check this journal!" The cadet turned to a ThinkPad that sat per-fectly aligned with other items on a small desk. "Here's today. See? The dentist appointment at 9:50. Now here's yesterday. Four appointments yesterday, and he's made comments after every one!"

Tony took a deep breath, held it, and exhaled. "I think, Cadet Fineberg, that for the present we should keep your perusal of the computer programs just between us. A small matter of a search warrant?" Before Rena could react she added, "Nevertheless, I rather think we'll be requesting one. You've done a good job, Fineberg; I'll tell the chief that, but you'll have to let the regulars take over now. Mr. Litt's sister has reason to worry. Looks to me like he definitely planned to come home after seeing the dentist."

What evidence leads Tony to believe Mr. Litt planned to come right back home after the dentist visit?

21

A COLUMBO CASE

Something I've noticed in my years with the coroner's office is that suicides are always discovered in the morning. Perhaps it's because the people who decide to end it all find it easier to do at night. Maybe in darkness it's easier to decide there's nothing to live for. Whatever the reasons—and there are reams of studies on the subject—the call I got this morning from Sergeant Rapathy is typical.

"Someone for your bailiwick," he bellowed. I don't know why, but on the phone he always shouts as if I'm at the bottom of a well. "One of our patrol guys found him this morning. Been dead a couple days judging by the stink. Up on The Bluffs. You know that little curvy road that runs from the park right to the edge of the cliff? The one with the fence across it that the kids keep taking down?"

I acknowledged that I did know the road. Said it as softly as I could, too, but he didn't take the hint. He never does.

"I've not done the scene myself. From what the uniform says it's gotta be a suicide, so I was thinkin' why don't you go on up, and if everything's kosher you can handle it directly 'cause it'll be coroner's office anyway. I'll let the uniform write it up and sign off from our end. Good experience for him."

We agreed on that, so after a bit more back and forth it wasn't long before I found myself on the way to The Bluffs. This is a pretty nice spot, actually. Sandstone cliffs that plunge right down to the shore of Lake Huron. Not huge, maybe four, five stories high but the wave action has eroded them into interesting shapes. At the far end, the south, there's a spit runs out and curls back on itself. It's the sheerest part of The Bluffs. Used to be a road along the top. Still is, unofficially, but it's barricaded now because a bunch of kids from the local high school went over the edge a couple of years ago. As you may have noted from what Rapathy said, the barrier doesn't last long.

I walked down the spit. Could have driven like the kids do, not to mention the suicide I was going to check on, but I figured somebody has to draw the line. The effort had made me puff a bit by the time I reached the car, even though it was a pretty cool day, so I leaned on the police cruiser for a few minutes, glad to rest while I got the details from the uniform who'd called it in. He's a new one. Nice kid.

From where I stopped, I could get much of the essential detail, and it sure looked like something I've seen before. More often than I care to. The car was driven right up to the very edge of the bluff, not head on but parallel, so close you could open the driver-side door and pitch right down to the lake without touching the ground. I'm no expert on cars, but it wasn't a new model. Actually looked a bit beat up. That afternoon I found out it was a renter from a discount outfit. I could see a hose, looked like plastic pipe—I've seen it before too, used for the same purpose—leading from the exhaust pipe to the rear window, passenger side. A healthy plastering of masking tape covered the crack, and all the other windows had masking tape around the edges.

The rookie cop warned me several times about the smell. I could make his skin crawl with some of the stuff that's gone past my nose, but I didn't say anything. He was just trying to be helpful. What I did, though, was open the passenger door wide and then step back. Opened the back door, too, for a little draft. The body was in the driver's seat. White male, about forty plus; average-average. No signs of trauma. For sure he'd shuffled off this mortal coil more than a day ago, but the body was still at that sweetish smell stage they have before decay really makes them reek.

I had to agree everything said suicide: the hose, the masking tape, ignition on, gas gauge showing empty. And, of course, the note. It was typed—"keyed" I guess is the word used now. At any rate, it came out of a printer. Now that was new to me. Every other one of these I've seen is handwritten. When we I.D.'d the guy a while later, we learned he owned a computer store, so keying a note would have been normal in his case, I guess. By the way, I should say used to own a computer store. Very successful one, too, but it was sold as part of a divorce settlement about a year and a half ago. Anyway, the whole package taken together made it look like the guy had rigged up his car for monoxide, driven up to The Bluffs, parked, and just let the motor run.

I took all the required pictures. Even thought of asking the kid if he wanted to come and pose, but thought better of it. That's the kind of thing the older, jaded cops do; he'll get there soon enough. But what I did do . . . this is kind of embarrassing really but . . . The thing is I used to be a real fan of Columbo. Remember the detective series with Peter Falk? A real classic. I watched it in black-and-white! There was this one show where a supposed suicide dies in his car. Columbo finds a bunch of cassettes in the car, all jazz, Bix Biederbecke and that, but when he turns on the car's radio he finds it's pre-tuned to stations that play only down-home country. That discrepancy leads Columbo to one thing and another until he solves the case. Turns out it wasn't suicide at all.

So I played Columbo! Always wanted to do that. I turned on the radio, and what did I hear? Classical! Even a tin ear can recognize Mozart. Of course, I immediately looked around for tapes and CDs, but there weren't any. Still, it was a start. The next thing to do was to find out if this station is classical full time —and find out if the recently deceased was a classical buff. I was just about to check the pre-tuned stations, when the rookie's shadow scared the daylights out of me.

"Your people are here from the morgue, Doctor Pelowich," he said. "They want to know if they can take the body."

Of course, I couldn't let them do that. Now that I was pretty sure it was a homicide, I'd have to get Sergeant Rapathy up here after all.

Doctor Pelowich hands the case back to the police because it's not a suicide. What is the clue that leads him to that conclusion?

—22—

THE CHASE

"Go ahead, six-two-three." The dispatcher's voice was neutral.

"We are in pursuit of a red pickup truck." Finn Sullivan spoke into the transmitter. "A Ford One-Fifty, traveling north on Hope Road. It just crossed Valley Line at . . . at 9:13."

Finn stole a quick glance at the speedometer. His partner's fingers were white on the steering wheel. "Stay cool," Finn said. "Just keep him in sight." He turned back to the transmitter. "Repeat! In pursuit of—"

"Got it all, six-two-three." The dispatcher broke in. "Sounds like that truck the APB is calling for. You want a block on Hope Road, Sully? Spike belt?"

For a split second, Finn was taken aback by the dispatcher's informality. The new superintendent was very strict about that kind of behavior. "No block until further advised," he said. "Repeat. No block! Can you put cars into the pursuit area?"

"I have twenty-one en route and four-oh-four. Estimate five minutes to intersection of Hope Road and Tecumseh Line." The dispatcher was more formal this time.

"Ten-four. Six-two-three will advise as needed." Finn dropped the transmitter into its cradle and tightened his seat belt as he peered into the distance. The red truck was widening the distance between them. "Was a time," he said as much to himself as to his partner, "when all the roads were dirt up here in the back country. All you had to do was follow dust."

"Well, there's no dust now." Ross Cawber replied. If he was trying to keep the tension out of his voice, he was not succeeding. "I'm being cool like you said, but he's gaining! Can only see him now when he tops a rise!"

"Just do it." Finn spoke very softly. "These roads up here are one hill after another, and full of bad curves. If he's a local, like we think, he knows them like the back of his hand. You and me, we go too fast on the right one, we'll go airborne. Or else we'll roll, so . . . "

The next minute passed in silence as the truck topped another rise in the distance. It was even farther ahead now.

Ross asked the obvious question: "What if he turns in somewhere?"

"Farm lanes are dirt and gravel," Finn replied. "We'd see the plume; he knows that. There's no way off Hope Road now until he gets over the top of Mount . . . ah . . . see? There he goes up Mount Skeena."

Ross pushed the accelerator harder as the two officers watched the truck. Mount Skeena was the dominant rise in this landscape full of hills, and Hope Road ran long and straight to the top. The truck was just seconds from the crest when the police car began its climb. Both men could hear the engine strain as the transmission dropped into progressively lower gears.

Ross kept the accelerator to the floor, but the road in front was empty when they reached the top. To make matters worse, it forked. He fought a fishtail as he braked to a stop, but he was still the first to notice a man and dog at the side of the road.

"There's a guy and a—!"

"I see him," Finn answered calmly. "Ask him, but go easy. From the overalls, I'd say he's local for sure. They don't much like us. Goes way back to the moonshine days."

Ross pulled over. The man was well past middle age and carted a huge stomach inside the overalls. He was in need of a shave. A bath, too, Ross concluded as he rolled down the window.

"There's a red truck . . . "

"Say 'Good day' first!" Finn hissed between his teeth.

Ross swallowed. "Good day, sir."

The man nodded. He stood very still, his shoulders drooping. One hand rested on the bib of his overalls. In the other, he held the dog's leash.

"A red truck come by here just now?"

The hand came off the overalls and went to rest on a hip. The other fell to the opposite hip. The man leaned back from the waist and gave out a long, slow sigh. "Yup," he said, and frowned and tipped his head as though the whole thing had been quite a novel experience. Then, after a long pause, he added, "Come up the hill myself just now, me 'n' the dog. Passed me in an awful hurry, he did. Went on down toward Cutter Creek there." He motioned to the left fork.

Ross nodded a thank you, accelerated, and turned the car to the left.

"Wait!" For the first time, Finn's voice betrayed excitement. "Go right! The right fork." Ross was about to argue, when Finn continued. "The other two cars are due in a minute or so; we'll send them to Cutter Creek. But our truck has gone to the right. I'm sure of it!"

"The old guy lied?" Ross asked. "How can you tell?"

"He told us too much." Finn said. "He's a plant. His job is to send us the wrong way."

Why does Finn believe "the old guy lied"?

—23—
THE KEY TO THE CODE

"Hurry up! You're supposed to be flipping through the books, not reading them!"

"I'm not reading them! Just the titles. This guy is a closet librarian. Look at how they're lined up! Baxter, A Professional Prepares for the Back Country; Meyer, Survival Tips; Moscovitz, Eating Off the Land; O'Connor, Equipment Essentials; and—ooh, this one must keep him up at night—Toselli, Mushrooms and Other Edible Fungi."

"That's what I mean. You're reading! Control said we've only got about an hour to find the key to this code system, so start flipping. The guy could be back any time."

"Yeah, yeah, yeah. It's just . . . I mean, look at these shelves, the way they're set up. The guy must have been toilet-trained too soon."

"What?"

"An old Freudian idea. If your parents are freaked on the potty thing and start you too early, you grow up wanting to have everything in neat little piles."

"Dumbest thing I ever heard!"

"Well, it explains this guy. I mean, look! Here's the survival books, all grouped. Empty space at the end, so he plans for the future, too. Jump to the next shelf for the wildflower guides; below that the bird books. Nature freak, that's for sure. Now, here's the hiking books: Dartmouth, Along the Bruce Trail; Gotha, Hiking the Spine of the Tetons; Nibor and Best, Vancouver Island's Best . . . the computer's beeping! Aren't we supposed to be in a hurry!"

"It's slow. His system is absolutely archaic. Kindergarten

level to penetrate, but it's a foot dragger. If the code key is in here, I'll find it easy enough, but ..."

"Well, so far there's nothing stuffed into any of these books ... Palgrave, Grand Canyon Trails ... he sure must be some hiker ... Van Buren, From the Blue Ridge to the Smokies ... Fredericks, Yellowstone's Best Day Hikes ... you sure Control said only an hour?"

"Control doesn't want the guy to know we're on to him. He's only a bit player, but the desk weenies at Langley are sure he's got the key to the code. Anyway, the surveillance team says an hour."

"I think he'll be gone for a lot longer than that. Audubon, Birds of America ... Wow! This is an original! A first printing!"

"Does it have the key to the code in it?"

"You have no soul, do you? Casey, West Coast Flyers; Lavenchuk, Birds of the Pacific Coast ... looks like he gets to the other end of the country once in a while ... Peterson, Field Guide to the Birds ... might have expected that one."

"Will you stop babbling and speed up! We're never going to—"

"I've got an idea!"

"Be the first time."

"No, no! Do this! Key in this file name: 'Dewey.' D-E-W-E-Y."

"Look, we haven't got time to—"

"Just do it!"

"Okay, Okay. D-E-W-E-Y. C'mon, c'mon. This thing is so slow! See? Nothing."

"All right, all right. Try ... er ... try 'Dewey System': D-E–"

"I know, I know . . . See? Nothing again. This is just holding things up. I'm going back to—"

"One more! Just one more. Try 'Dewey Classification System.'"

"Too big. Too long. I'll try 'DSC' and see what comes u—. Holy Cow! Look at the data! Reams of it!"

"I knew it! The way this guy is organized, it had to be. See, in the Dewey system, non-fiction books are grouped by subject, just like he's got them here. And what he's done, he's catalogued and classified them in that file like a library would. A backup, I suppose, or maybe he just likes to do it."

"So Dewey was toilet-trained early too, huh? By the way, why did we just do this?"

"I'll give you whatever odds you want that the key to the code is buried in there with all those words and numbers. It'll take some time to figure it out, but it's gotta be in that 'DSC' file there. Copy it to a floppy."

"Floppy drive doesn't work. I found that out first thing."

"So print it. We'll take a hard copy."

"Have you seen that printer? It's a dot matrix. An old dot matrix! We'll be here forever!"

"Doesn't matter."

"What do you mean?"

"I say we've got a lot more than an hour. If I'm right, this guy is gone for days, maybe longer."

On what evidence does the last speaker base his theory that "this guy is gone for days, maybe longer"?

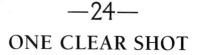

—24—
ONE CLEAR SHOT

The man alighting from a hansom cab in London's Knightsbridge Road had all the appearance of a proper gentleman. The demeanor, however, was slightly off—the way the cane was held, for example, and the angle of the hat. Not overt enough for anyone to notice unless particular attention was paid, and, fortunately for the man, no one in this part of Knightsbridge—no one who mattered—would ever do anything that vulgar. Still, the porter at the Wellington Club caught it. Not that he would ever say anything. But his was a practiced eye; he could spot a pretender in a single glance. The waiter in the Raleigh Room caught it too; he'd been at The Wellington even longer than the porter but, like his confrere, knew the importance of discreet silence. When the stranger announced he was a guest of Mr. D'Arcy Jerome, both men treated him with the same deference that they showed the members.

D'Arcy Jerome, on the other hand, was less careful to conceal his opinions. "Don't use a cane," he said as soon as the two of them were seated at an alcove table in the Raleigh Room. "Or else learn to use it properly. You look like a colonial. Or an American."

The guest, whose name was Rodney Firth, bristled slightly and might have offered a retort had the waiter not appeared just then with a decanter of claret. A good thing, too, for his temper had cost him in the past and this was not a job he wanted to lose. Two thousand pounds and a pleasant sail to India and back, just for popping off this snob Jerome's even snobbier wife. It was worth swallowing a bit of pride.

The hint of anger faded even more quickly when D'Arcy Jerome moved his glass to one side and set down a small folder. It was neatly tied with narrow brown ribbon.

"One thousand pounds," D'Arcy said.

Rodney was envious of the way such a sum could be spoken so casually.

"Half now, as agreed." D'Arcy poked at the folder in a derisive way with one finger. "And your ticket on the Star of Mombasa. She sails for Bombay on the twenty-first. That's in two days. You are on the First Deck in Suite 1-A. That's on the port side. When you reach Bombay, the Mombasa will dock right beside the Star of Mandalay, so you will be directly opposite Mrs. Jerome's stateroom. She will be on Mandalay's First Deck, but on the starboard side. No question she'll be aboard." He paused and allowed himself a slight smirk. "She'd sooner die than miss Queen Victoria's jubilee celebrations. They begin in a month or so."

"What if her porthole windows are closed?" Rodney ventured. A reasonable concern, he thought, but D'Arcy's reaction suggested otherwise.

"In Bombay?" D'Arcy fixed Rodney with a cold stare. "Bombay, India? In July?" He flicked a manicured fingernail against his wineglass, and the waiter appeared out of the shadows to pour the claret. When they were alone again, D'Arcy continued, his manner indicating that whatever flaws Rodney might find in the plan, he should keep them to himself.

"As I said, when she reaches Bombay, the Mombasa will dock directly beside her sister ship. They will lie side by side for about twenty-four hours before the Mandalay sets sail for England. You'll be in one of the noisiest harbors in the world, so it's not likely a shot will be heard." Then he added, "One shot."

D'Arcy held his wine to the light as though its color and texture were more important at this moment than the imminent dispatching of his wife. He put it down and returned to the stare. "I can guarantee you at least two opportunities over that time period. Agatha is nothing if not boringly consistent. The first will be in late morning. She will stroll the deck after breakfast, then return to her dressing room to repair herself following such incredibly exhausting activity. The maid will let down her hair and then leave her to rest. This procedure will be repeated after the luncheon. Her steward, incidentally, will be busy the entire day attending to last-minute details below deck. If you take the shot in the morning and then leave, you won't likely see him at all."

D'Arcy lifted his eyebrows to indicate that Rodney could ask questions now if he wished, but Rodney had resolved to carry the rest of this through with his dignity intact, and remained silent.

"There is one . . . " D'Arcy sat a little straighter in his chair and said, "I'm told, Mr. Frith . . . er . . . Firth, that you have more than a little . . . er . . . expertise in this field?"

Rodney raised one eyebrow the tiniest bit. He felt just a little weight shifting to his side for a change.

"Because there will be no second opportunity," D'Arcy carried on. "It will require a single, perfect shot. You will be well positioned in Suite 1-A; these are precisely identical ships. But there is the matter of the angle."

Rodney smiled confidently. He knew what D'Arcy Jerome meant. "Just have the other half ready, sir," he said. "The other thousand, I mean."

D'Arcy Jerome knows that Frith will be shooting at an angle. Why, if the ships are identical, will this be necessary?

—25—
BLANK WITNESSES

Mrs. Corinne Wilson sat precisely in the center of a rattan armchair, with every limb poised. Her legs were crossed just so at the knees, her hands folded and resting in her lap, and her head was tilted a few demure degrees to the left. To Officer Marni Dreyfuss, the lady was a logo for the neighborhood: ordered, neat, proper—and gated.

The clothes matched the posture for, like the houses and gardens in Oxford Manor, Corinne Wilson was a product of professional design. Her shoes were soft brown suede, open-toed with a wedge-type sole, perfect for a sunny weekday morning in early fall. So was the mid-calf skirt, cotton with a mix of lighter browns and white, along with a touch or two of olive green. A white blouse with mother-of-pearl buttons was quietly elegant under the sweater that hung with artful casualness over her shoulders. It was a cashmere sweater, olive green.

Oxford Manor itself was not a row of mansions, any more than Corinne Wilson was a millionaire, but it was an expensive neighborhood: sophisticated, definitely high-end. And filled with people interested in keeping things that way. In her uniform, somewhat disheveled now six hours into her shift, Marni Dreyfuss looked like an intruder. Which, in effect, she was. Not many uniformed police officers were seen here in the daytime, and never on a 9-1-1 assault call. The 9-1-1 had been passed to Marni and her partner an hour ago, just as they cruised into a Denny's parking lot. They'd been on duty since 3:00 and had just told the dispatcher they were taking twenty for breakfast when they were tabbed. It was a domestic, the kind of call every patrol cop hates. Some guy was beating his wife on the front lawn of their house.

So far, everything had gone wrong. The caller—a female voice—had used a cellphone to blurt out an address and a "Hurry, he'll kill her!" and had then cut out. No identification; no trace possible. The guard at the gate had been a pain, dragging his feet about raising the bar. Then when Marni finally found Ashburnham Avenue after two wrong turns and pulled up to number 15, the house was empty. No one around—neither the alleged beater nor the alleged victim.

At this point, their tempers already frayed, Marni and her partner ran up against a succession of what their sergeant always referred to as "blank witnesses." They caught up with a postie at the end of the street, for example, and from the way he refused to meet Marni's eyes she knew he had something to offer, but all he would say is, "Look . . . I didn't see anything. I just deliver the mail."

Across the street at number 16, it was no better.

"We just got up a few minutes ago. We've no idea what you're talking about," a woman in a kimono told them, her mouth level with the chain that kept the door from opening more than a crack. A tall man stood behind her silently nodding. He was dressed, Marni noted.

They'd split up then, she and her partner, to canvass both sides of the street. Back in the alley behind number 17, the man Marni spoke to in his garage didn't try to be secretive, but he hadn't seen anything. Marni could understand why. Garages in Oxford Manor, along with garbage pails, lawn-mowers, and other detritus of suburban life, were kept properly out of sight behind the houses in alleyways. The design price that was paid for that feature was a pair of sidewalks at right-angles by the front door of every house. One led out to the street and the other branched left and then around the side to the alley. Unless he came right up his sidewalk from the alley, the man from number 17 couldn't see his own frontyard, much less the one at number 15.

"I've been back here quite a while," the man freely acknowledged. "Since maybe 7:00 or so. I'm an early riser, especially on these sunny fall days. Air is so nice and fresh, heavy dew sparkling on the lawns. Got to take advantage, I always say. Winter'll be here before you know it."

To Marni's next question he'd replied, "Yeah, maybe. I thought I heard voices or something out on the street around that time, but I'm not sure. Had my radio on, you see."

At that point Marni was ready to pack it in and, depending what her partner was turning up on the other side of the street, was thinking of maybe writing up a "dud" report on the 9-1-1 and calling it a day. Then the man added, "Saw Mrs. Wilson outside this morning around that time. She's number 19 next door. Maybe she can tell you something. Doesn't miss much." And that explained why, at this moment, Marni Dreyfuss was sitting on Corinne Wilson's front porch.

When she answered her front door, Mrs. Wilson's body language expressed discomfort, which Marni figured was because the lady couldn't decide whether it was proper to invite a police officer in, or whether she should allow herself to be interviewed standing in the doorway. The front porch was a compromise. Once she had properly positioned herself in the rattan chair, Mrs. Wilson opened by expressing curiosity about why a police officer could possibly want to speak to her. She pointedly added that she would be leaving in twenty-one minutes for the weekly meeting of the Literary Society.

Marni went straight to the point, told her about the 9-1-1 call, and said, "Number 17—Mr. Gomes, right?—he doesn't have a fence or a hedge, and number 15 doesn't either, so you have a clear view of both frontyards from the porch here, don't you?"

Corinne Wilson drew the sweater tighter.

"And, according to Mr. Gomes, you were out early this morning, around the time of the . . . er . . . reported incident. If the situation was serious enough to attract an emergency call, surely you must have seen or heard something. It's a very quiet neighborhood."

The hands came off the sweater and the fingers began to intertwine. Corinne Wilson leaned forward until the morning sunlight caught silver lights in her hair. There had been a rinse at work, Marni could see, but an expensive one. No blue shine on this lady.

"I was . . . yes, indeed, I was awake and dressed early. My meeting, you know. And yes, I was outside as Edward . . . Mr. Gomes said."

"So you must have seen something at number 15, Mrs. Wilson! Or heard something!" Marni's frustration was sitting right between them now.

Corinne Wilson leaned forward a bit more and turned her head. She raised a thin index finger until it rested on the tiny diamonds in her earlobe. "I only just put these in as you knocked. I never use them unless I go out."

It took Marni a few seconds to figure out that the older lady was talking about hearing aids. She had one in each ear.

"I don't confide this to anyone usually," she continued, "but I really don't hear much without them." For the first time, she smiled, a soft smile, not gentle so much as genteel. "The neighbors, the Fawcetts in 15 . . . yes, it's possible I may have seen them very briefly. But, you see, there was this sheet of old newspaper." Clearly, to Mrs. Wilson the unwelcome presence of the litter was on the level of mortal sin. "On my lawn! Breeze brought it in, I suppose. I went to get it, and actually had to chase it down between my house and the Taylors'—they're number 21." She pointed to the house on the right. "Took it right to the bin in the back, of course; I suppose that may be when Mr. Gomes saw me. And then I came in through my back door. So, you see, if the Fawcetts were out, I wouldn't have seen them, turned the other way as I was."

Whether it was the buildup of evasions that did it, or being just plain tired at the end of her shift—whatever the cause, Marni lost her cool.

"Mrs. Wilson!" she said, far louder than she wanted to. "Do you see that police officer across the street? That male police officer? He's my partner. Now you might have been able to fool him with a story like that, but not me. Not another woman!"

Marni Dreyfuss feels that being a woman has given her an edge in figuring out that Mrs. Wilson has lied to her. What part of Corinne Wilson's story does not ring true to her?

—26—
"FOR WANT OF A NAIL . . . "

T.G. Binkley felt a clammy grip of despair in his gut when he saw the green Honda Civic round the curve. He focused hard on the driver's face, just in case the desert heat was playing tricks with his eyesight, but it was Turgeon behind the wheel.

Had he been a violent man he might have slammed his fist into something, or shot off the big ugly Magnum he carried on his hip, but T.G. was not that kind. He was a planner: patient and careful. Those who saw only his outward side thought him a plodder, and not a very bright one at that. But T.G. Binkley had just carried off a heist that could well mean the corporate demise of Banko Armored Car Service. Well, almost carried off.

Twenty million dollars . . . and everything had gone perfectly, especially the trickiest part, the detour and the holdup! When the armored car left Salt Lake, going south on I-15 toward Provo, T.G. had maneuvered things so that he was driving. That way, one of the other two guards had taken over the wheel after the pickup in Provo, while T.G. moved over to the front passenger seat where he would be in charge of the radio. He and the other two had been using this rotating system for so long it had become automatic; no matter what the travel distance, at each stop they rotated clockwise one position. Neither of the other two was even aware of just how or when the rotation had become a system; that's how carefully and patiently T.G. worked.

South of Provo, the radio message had come right on schedule and it was T.G. who received. "Divert to Eureka and Hinckley for unscheduled pickups."

T.G. pretended to be as surprised as his two colleagues at the instruction, for it was not standard procedure. Not only that, it would mean driving a short stretch through the Sevier Desert, which was out of radio range. Still, the instruction came from Aurelia back at headquarters in Salt Lake—"Sister Aurelia," she called herself—and she had used all the proper codes, so they turned off the interstate.

The pickup at Eureka took only a short time, but it created another rotation, so that ten minutes later T.G. was in the back when they came upon the state trooper blocking the road. The trooper sent the armored car lumbering down a one-lane track in the desert that would, so she said, take them around the chemical spill ahead.

Things had gone so smoothly by now that T.G. was really not surprised when the truly dicey part, the holdup, went off as if rehearsed. A log across the track had forced the vehicle to stop, and before anyone could react T.G. had opened the back door. A complete violation of regulations, but the jig was up now anyway. A tall man in a ski mask appeared from the brush and pointed an armor-piercing weapon at the two guards in front, while T.G. tossed out the loot. Twenty million dollars evenly split between used tens and twenties! That's what Sister Aurelia had said was in this load. T.G. had subtly wooed the lonely and unattractive woman for a year.

It took a bit of time to empty the armored car, but that was in the plan. The bandit in the ski mask then used hand signals to tell the driver he had ten seconds to back up, drive around the log, and get going. As the sound of the engine faded in a cloud of dust, T.G. allowed himself a small smile.

This was Wednesday. On Wednesdays and Fridays he was responsible for gassing up and checking the gauges. Now all that was left was to get to the safe house, dole out the promised million each to his two new partners, set aside the same amount for Aurelia, and then . . . Panama!

The fading sound of the armored car was immediately replaced by the sound of Turgeon driving up. She'd gotten rid of the state trooper uniform, and although T.G. couldn't see, he was positive she was wearing the extremely tight shorts she always favored. The shorts had caused the only really serious argument during the planning process, because T.G. felt a car thief should realize how much attention they attracted.

On the other hand, Turgeon had accepted the logic of a "fresh scoop": that she would have to steal a car that very morning so it stood a better chance of being unreported while they drove to the safe house. And when T.G. had instructed her to pick a vehicle that would not attract attention—they certainly could not use the fake patrol car—she had simply nodded in agreement. On the issue of the shorts, however, T.G. knew Turgeon would do whatever she pleased no matter what he said.

"It's fresh," Turgeon said proudly, jerking a thumb at the windshield as she got out of the car, "Right out of long-term parking at the airport in Salt Lake."

T.G. couldn't help but notice she was wearing slacks, but the realization softened his despair for no more than a second. What he was thinking in his patient, methodical way was that it takes only one glitch to ruin a perfect crime.

What is the glitch that has ruined this "perfect crime"?

—27—
ONE WAY TO
BREAK UP A GLOOMY DAY

Mary Margaret O'Rourke stared through the large plate-glass window at the McDonald's wrapper floating along in the gutter. Its drift was erratic, for every few seconds a gust of wind would push it off course or a passing car would create little ripples that shifted it to one side or another. Mary Margaret watched it gloomily, wondering if the haphazard progress of the flimsy piece of waxed paper was a metaphor for her own life. Then, just as she concluded it probably was, two guys from the furniture store next door confirmed it. They were carrying a couch out to their delivery truck, and the leading man tromped the paper with a large booted foot, completely unaware he'd done so. Crushed now and more compact, the wrapper regained the surface and, floating a bit faster, snagged briefly on the furniture truck's rear tires before disappearing.

Mary Margaret lifted her chin in the direction of the paper and pressed her lips together. That was her life right now, she thought: drifting along, pushed and pulled and trampled, en route to somewhere but never in control.

"Maybe it's the rain," she said out loud, wondering if bad weather for the past two days had brought on such gloom.

"You say something?" It was Ellie, leaning over her desk at the back of the narrow room.

Mary Margaret whipped around. Ellie was supposed to be on her way to the county clerk's office. "No . . . er . . . noth—. What are you doing back here? Aren't you going to—?"

Ellie didn't wait. She never did. From the doorway she waved an umbrella. "Forgot this! I'm late—gotta hustle! See you tomorrow!"

Ellie was as bouncy and forward as Mary Margaret was introspective and private. That was why Ellie's desk was at the back of the room: so she would be the first person their drop-in clients would encounter. The two young women shared a common hallway with the discount furniture store next door and, to get into their tiny law office from the street, clients had to come in through that hallway. After an abrupt right turn through a door badly in need of paint, Ellie's bright smile was the first thing they saw.

Mary Margaret returned to the comfort of her gloom. Yes, the rain. That had to be part of it. And Peter. She hadn't told Ellie yet that she and Peter were finished. He'd simply walked out. She'd known it was coming; they'd gone over it a hundred times, and he just didn't get it. She wanted a career. And no matter how often—

A loud boom made her grab instinctively for her coffee cup, although it had been drained hours ago. Normally, she'd have cursed under her breath—never mind what her mother and the nuns might think—but today she didn't have the spirit for it. Besides, somewhere in her subconscious, she'd been expecting it. Whenever the furniture guys loaded up there were booms: sharp, loud, thumping bangs on the wall between her office and the common hallway. Sometimes they were forceful enough to spill her coffee if the cup was full. It was partly her fault, Mary Margaret knew. She had deliberately placed her desk as close to the front window as possible, and tight against the hallway wall. That way, by leaning forward and craning to her left she could see the one encouraging spot in this blighted area of the city: a tiny park across the street, where a few trees stubbornly offered colors other than gray. In winter, when the sun set early—that is, when the sun bothered to shine—she could watch it go down through the branches.

The downside to all this was the booming. Supposedly, the furniture guys accidentally bumped into the wall with their awkward loads, but Mary Margaret suspected it was a little more planned than that, for it had almost never happened until two of the younger types next door had come into the office one day and noticed where she had put her desk.

There was a second boom and then a third. Now it was becoming annoying! Mary Margaret was getting up to give the furniture guys a piece of her mind, when she heard them shouting out on the street. She knew right away what this would be about, and, with both depression and annoyance temporarily forgotten, went to see the street from a better angle. Sure enough, her neighbors were having another round in their ongoing fight with Melnick's Used Electronics.

Melnick's was across the street and two doors north of the furniture store. Mary Margaret didn't like the people there. In fact she was just a bit afraid of them. After she'd represented a client against them and won, one of the Melnicks had let her know what he thought of her "meddling" and of lawyers in general, especially women. The furniture store didn't like them either because the two businesses were in constant dispute about parking their respective trucks on the narrow street. Melnick's had a big, battered old flatbed truck that somehow was always parked at a protruding angle with the back end far from the curb, thus making it even more difficult to bring the large furniture van along the curb on the opposite side. As a result, there was a tangle of some kind at least once a week. No big deal, though: in this part of the city shouts and fights were a way of life.

To Mary Margaret, this particular episode didn't seem to be going anywhere, but along with the booms it had shaken her mood enough to make her feel that a fresh cup of coffee might help her get some work done. It was while she was in the back, in front of the coffee machine— something else they shared with the furniture guys—that Melnick's aged truck smashed right through the plate-glass window and into her desk.

Mary Margaret dashed back to the office, but wisely stopped in the doorway. Through the dust, she could see that the big window was shattered, but what was really scary was the position of the truck. The edge of its flatbed platform covered her desk like a big blotter. Had she not gone for coffee . . .

She became conscious of excited voices. All the furniture guys came rushing in. Some came from the back; others she could see squeezing in through the space the truck had left at the street door. Above all the noise she could hear Ellie.

"Omigod! Are you all right? I thought for sure you . . .

Omigod! I was right out there on the street! That stupid old truck! And the way they always park! The brakes must have failed, and it rolled right across. Or else—you know what? I bet those clods never even set the parking brake ... Omigod! We've got to go after them. That's a felony! Criminal neglect, at least, probably more!"

"Much more!" Mary Margaret's voice made it clear that her gloom had been firmly pushed aside. "Assault. Assault with intent! That was no failed brakes affair."

Mary Margaret is right. Why could this not have been a "failed brakes affair"?

A PERFECT WITNESS

"What I don't understand, young lady, is why I have to go over all this again. I told the officers at the accident what I saw, and they wrote it all down."

"Yes, I understand, sir, but that was—"

"Father."

"I beg your pardon?"

"Father. I'm a priest. I'd prefer you address me as 'Father.'"

"Of course, I'm sorry. Now the reason we have to go over this again, Father . . . er . . . Belcher, the reason we're doing it again is because, if this goes to trial, I will be prosecuting the case, and the fact is, I really need to be familiar with everything you might say as a witness."

"Hmpf." Father Leonard Belcher took off his glasses and began to polish them furiously with the torn lining of his suit coat. "Very well. What do you need to know that isn't on the police report? That's what's on your desk there, isn't it? I noticed it when I came in."

"Yes, I have the report. But let's go back to the—"

"You know, I really should have your surname. I can't be calling you 'Serena.' Not proper, in my opinion."

There was a pause. "It's Gelberg."

"Very well. Miss Gelberg."

"Ms."

"Indeed. Ms. Gelberg." Father Belcher polished even harder and fixed his gaze on the ceiling. Serena, meanwhile, looked down at the report, running her fingernail very slowly down the edge of the police report as though looking for something specific. When she felt the air had thinned a bit, she started again.

"As I understand it, Father Belcher, you were standing on the northwest corner of Brock and Prevost when the accident happened?"

"Yes, I was reading my office." The priest folded his glasses in one hand and leaned forward. His tone became soft and conspiratorial. "I'd almost forgotten it! Still had a page or so left, and the light was beginning to fade."

Serena looked confused. "I'm sorry . . . your 'office'?"

"A daily reading. From this." With some difficulty Father Belcher extracted a leather-bound breviary from his suit coat pocket. "It's required. Some of the young priests don't bother to do it every day, but I—"

"So, you were reading your . . . er . . . office when the car rolled over in the intersection?"

"Yes. I didn't see the beginning of things, but I heard a very loud bang. I think the car hit something. I didn't see what—I told the police officer that—but the noise caught my attention, and I turned and saw the car roll over. I think it would have rolled again, but it came to rest against the lamppost kitty-corner from me."

"The southeast corner."

"Yes."

"And you saw the driver, Mr. de Leon, get out of the car?"

"Almost right away he got out. The car was upside down, but the door was wide open. I could smell alcohol."

"You could smell alcohol from the opposite corner?"

"No, when I crossed the street. Like I said, he got out and leaned against the car. I went over to him then and asked, 'Are you all right?'; that's when I could smell the alcohol."

Serena ran her fingernail down the report again. "The investigating officer wrote here that you said, 'Are you okay?'"

"No, I said, 'Are you all right?' I have a very good memory."

Serena handed the report to the priest. "The bottom of the page," she said. "Your words are in quotation marks, and ... er ... aren't those your initials in the margin?"

The priest said "Hmpf" twice into the ensuing silence before handing the report back. "Yes, perhaps I did say 'okay.' But surely that's a trivial matter!"

"Indeed it is," Serena agreed, nodding her head. "But the defense will have a copy of this report, too, and it's important that what you say on the witness stand ... well, no matter for the moment. The truly vital issue is this passenger you saw get out of the car. That's what the defense will be after and, quite frankly, it's what may take this case beyond a drunk-driving charge into a whole other issue. Now you're absolutely certain, Father Belcher, you saw a passenger, an adolescent, a female adolescent?"

"I know what I saw. Before he—this Mr. de Leon—was even on his feet, a young girl crawled out the back window on the other side of the car. Mr. de Leon said, 'I think you better go make a phone call fast,' and then she disappeared. Don't ask me where she went."

"Please understand if I press you on this, because de Leon swears there was nobody else in the car. And he told the officer he said, 'I think I better go make a phone call fast.' You know, don't you—well, I'm sure you do—that nobody else saw a passenger? But, then, you're the only eyewitness—at least so far, although I doubt any more are going to show up."

"I know what I saw."

The attorney tugged at her straight black hair. "Just now you said 'young girl,' yet in the report you—"

"Yes, yes, I know. I just read it. To the policeman I said 'young adolescent.' You have no idea, Ms. Gelberg, how all this politically correct nonsense has made the language confusing for people of my generation. Is it okay to call a woman a 'girl,' for example? When is 'female' the right word? And this he/she drivel! But that's beside the point. I know what I saw. Now, could I pick this . . . this young person out of a line-up of others her age and size? Not with certainty, unless she happens to be wearing the peculiar little necklace she had on at the time of the accident. Do I know her? No. Have I ever seen her before? Not that I know of. How old was she? I wouldn't venture to say, but definitely under sixteen. Now, does that help?"

"Very emphatic, very emphatic." Serena looked at her watch. "And I thank you for being so cooperative. Not least for taking the time to come in."

Father Belcher recognized a termination signal, for he'd used similar ones many times himself. He stood and put on his glasses, straightened his suit coat, and offered his hand across the desk.

Serena Gelberg smiled. "Now that's politically correct, Father Belcher! Let me guess: when you were my age you shook hands only with men. Am I right?"

The priest smiled in return. He felt he could get to like this young lady. As he reached the door, he paused for a second with one hand on the doorknob. The smile was still on his face.

"Tell me, Ms. Gelberg. You're Jewish, right?"

"Yes."

"When you talk to your rabbi, you address him as 'Rabbi,' don't you?"

"Well, the fact is I'm not . . . well, yes, I do. Why do you ask?"

"Just curious; just curious. Nothing more."

The telephone rang on Serena's desk just as the door closed behind the priest. It was her department head, and she knew exactly what the call was about.

"No, darn it," she said, even before she was asked, "not a perfect witness. If the defence has him read something they will definitely be able to weaken his testimony."

What has Serena noted that may weaken Father Belcher's value as a witness?

—29—
ACCIDENTAL DEATH?

<small>Belfountain Life & Indemnity Incorporated</small>

July 10, 1968

Mr. Alberto Cantella
Roshmon, Cantella, Burns & Habib
51st Floor, Caledon Place
King City

Dear Mr. Cantella,

I am replying to your letter of May 28, 1968, in which you inform us that you now represent the estate of Xavier P.B. Lutz.

To answer your questions in order:

1. Briefly, the circumstances of Mr. Lutz's death are as follows: On September 22, 1965, at 9:30 A.M., the body of the deceased was discovered on the second-level landing of a stairwell in the Palgrave Underground Parking Garage. According to the report of the medical examiner, death occurred between 10:00 P.M. and midnight the previous day. This report also states that Mr. Lutz died instantly of a single gunshot wound to the heart from a .32 caliber bullet. Evidence indicates that two weapons were used at the crime scene and three shots were fired. A gun with the deceased's fingerprints on it was found near the body. This weapon, also .32 caliber, was the property of Mr. Lutz and was duly registered. It had been fired twice, and the spent bullets were found in the stairwell.

The weapon used to kill Mr. Lutz was never found.

On the second anniversary of the incident, September 21, 1967, the police department acknowledged that it had not been able to identify a suspect in the shooting of Mr. Lutz, and that it had transferred the case to its "cold files."

2. The late Mr. Lutz was the owner of whole life policy #97352 with Belfountain Life & Indemnity. The policy has a face value of $100,000 with a double indemnity clause in the event of accidental death, raising face value in such a situation to $200,000.

3. On September 30, 1967, following the announcement of the police force with regard to the investigation, Belfountain Life & Indemnity issued a cheque for $100,000 to the estate of Mr. Lutz.

4. It is the position of the firm that the particulars in this case do not constitute "accidental death," as defined by the Insurance Act and that, as a consequence, the double indemnity clause does not apply. As stipulated in Section IV(b) ix, of the Federal Insurance Act, a death by murder is regarded as "accidental death" for insurance purposes, provided that at the time of, or immediately prior to, the death the victim is not engaged in activity that is provocative, in whole or in part, of the circumstances leading to the death.

I trust the above is the information you seek.

Yours sincerely,

J. Piers Cutter, V.P. Settlement

Belfountain Life & Indemnity Inc

Why does the insurance company not regard Mr. Lutz's death as "accidental" for insurance purposes?

—30—
IT'S ELEMENTARY

Anyway, that's the good part. About being a cop, I mean. As for the bad part ... I've only been out of the academy three months now and the stuff that bugs the older ones, you know, shift work and that, it just doesn't bother me. Least not yet, anyway. But ... okay, there's one thing. One really big thing, actually. See, my name is Watson. My surname. Yeah, you can tell what's coming already, can't you? Now, you may not think it's such a big deal, and I'll grant you, the first time somebody on the force said, "elementary, my dear Watson," to me, I just shrugged it off. After all, I am the junior member here, and I suppose it's to be expected. But try putting up with it every day, on every case, on every call!

Like the other morning, when I went out with "Domie" Karges on this shooting investigation. Oh . . . maybe I should explain that we're a pretty small rural police force. Not a lot of major crime here, so we don't go out in pairs except when there's a specific thing to look into. Then the sheriff just partners up whoever's around. I'd signed in early that morning, so I guess he picked me 'cause I was standing closest. Tells me I'm going out on this shooting thing, and then sends me out to the garage to roust Domie.

Domie is one of the old guys, a veteran. There's one like him in every police station, I guess. Not a bad guy, and not stupid or anything like that, but lazy. And senior enough to know where all the bodies are buried, so he can get away with snoozing on the old car seats out back. Out

116

of everyone on the force from the sheriff on down, Domie's the worst for the "elementary, my dear Watson" thing.

Anyway, the shooting. We've got this big game farm just off the highway west of town. Some rich guy from Calgary owns it. Full of elk and buffalo and some exotic stuff like eland and gemsbok. Big, high, chain-link fence around it. The farm's not a real big problem for anybody but us. (Well, maybe it is for the animal rights types. There's a few of them show up twice, three times a year with placards and hand out pamphlets.) But for us it's a real pain. You see, we've got our share of yahoos in the county—doesn't everybody?—and of course, they've all got rifle racks, and this game farm—well, it's like waving a red flag. Those animals weren't out there a week before we had our first incident. Like the sheriff says, "It's Newton's fourth law: a yahoo's got a gun, he's gonna kill something."

So, first thing I did that morning was go get Domie like I was supposed to, and sure enough he was snoring away out in the garage. He's got a great set of antennae though. Before I even opened my mouth, he says, "Did you check that there's snowshoes in the trunk? If we're gonna go out there to see where the shooter was standing, we may need 'em. Snow's still pretty deep."

I guess I must have looked a bit confused, because he went on.

"This is about the game farm thing, right? The shot yesterday? I was the one who took the call, shortly after noon. Farm manager heard a shot and ran out. One a' those big African things—what's it called, eland?—was stumbling around, bleeding. Then he calls us."

The explanation continued in the car. I drove.

"Nobody else around, so I went out alone. By the time I got there, the vet had already been and gone, and the animal's still alive! Bullet went right through it."

Now, it's probably my own fault for giving him the opportunity, because I asked, "How could that happen?"

"Elementary ballistics, my dear Watson. Shooter used a military round, a hard-nose bullet. The movies like to call it 'full metal jacket.' Sexier, I guess. Anyway it went right through the beast. Now a hunter . . . a hunter'd use a soft-nose, so's it could blow a real hole open and stay inside. Kills fast and sure."

I knew I was risking another jab, but I asked if that helped him figure out where the shooter must have been standing and was that why we needed snowshoes. To go out to the spot and take a look.

"Yeah, from the entry and exit wounds, and the hoofprints and blood spots that showed where the thing was standing, the shot had to come from the south. Watch the road!"

I'd been keen to blurt out a name and had fishtailed a bit on a piece of black ice in my excitement. "Hank Lipsett," I finally said.

Domie just nodded. Now, any other case I'd have scored a point or two with that call, but this guy Lipsett, he's on the list every time there's an unexplained shooting. Real gun nut, and a yahoo's yahoo. Even the army didn't want him. They'd parted company some years back—one of those 'if you leave voluntarily, then we won't kick you out' deals. I don't have all the details.

Domie stretched a bit. "Lipsett's place is first one south a' the game farm," he said, "so he's a suspect, no matter what. And we know he loads his own ammo. Don't know why. Probably stole enough from the army to fight a war."

I was driving slower now since the fishtail. Besides, I was ready to hear more.

"Went over to his place then, straight from the game farm," Domie went on. "Says he heard a shot all right. Earlier in the day, when he was in the barn. From the sound, he figures it was a .30-06 or maybe a .303. He oughta know; he's got both. But here's the thing!"

Domie straightened right up in the seat. Not like him at all. If I didn't know better, I'd have thought he was excited. "Lipsett, he volunteers that he went over there. Over to the game farm, I mean. To the fence to have a look-see. But not till later; in fact, he said he'd just got back when I drove in."

"And it was getting dark by then," I chimed in before Domie could point out the obvious. "Too late for you to go out and see for yourself, and that's why we're going now."

As it turned out, we didn't need the snowshoes. There'd been two, three clear days in a row with bright spring sun and then real cold nights, so, deep as it was, the snow was packed pretty solid, and we were there early enough in the day to be able to walk on top of it without sinking in. There were several sets of tracks along the south side of the big chain-link fence, but it didn't take more than about ten minutes before we came on a single set leading from Lipsett's barn and back again.

"Greb," I said, after I'd crouched down to look at the boot treads. They were in pretty deep. "'Bout size 11 or 12, I'd say. That'd be about Lipsett's size, wouldn't it?"

Domie didn't answer at first. He was a couple of steps farther along, down on one knee, his nose pretty close to the snow. "A .30-06, unless I miss my guess," he said.

He was staring at a shell casing, a couple, maybe three inches below the surface. I have to admit I'm not sure I would have seen it.

"We better get a picture before I dig it out." He was all business. "The boot tracks, too. No matter that everybody's got Grebs this year after the sale at Wal-Mart."

"Then what?" I asked. "Go confront Hank?"

Of course, it happened again. I know, I know . . . it was my own fault. What's so irritating is that, even as it was coming out of my mouth, I clued in that whoever shot the eland, it wasn't Hank Lipsett. But that didn't stop Domie from shaking his head like I'm some kind of idiot, or stop him either from saying, "Missed some elementary stuff, my dear Watson, didn't you?"

What elementary clues did Watson miss that point to Hank Lipsett's likely innocence in this shooting? (There are at least three.)

— 31 —
A SECOND INVESTIGATION
AT BEDSIDE MANOR

F reddy Scolino was one of those New Yorkers who believed that anybody going too far above Yonkers would fall off the edge of the earth. His wife had once explained to her relatives upstate that Freddy never came with her on visits because being more than a block from a subway station gave him a nervous rash. So when he announced at the beginning of August that he thought he might go with her for a few days at her brother Cosmo's place up in the Finger Lakes district, she was speechless. The surprise also made her very agreeable, and when Cosmo's next-door neighbor, some guy from Immigration, showed up unannounced on the second day to ask if Freddy Scolino, the cop, would help him with something just a few miles away, she was quite content to let him get involved.

The "something" was a week-old burglary at Bedside Manor, an old woolen mill converted into a high-priced bed and breakfast by a pair of young entrepreneurs from Freddy's own turf.

"Spent a fortune, those two kids," Lawrence, the Immigration guy, explained on the short drive over. "Must have parents with deep pockets. Mind you, they charge an arm and a leg, too."

Lawrence spent more time describing the renovations to the old mill—how they had rebuilt the water wheel and had it working and so on—than he did telling Freddy why he wanted a New York cop to come with him. Eventually, it came out that the local police had investigated the burglary, and Lawrence wasn't too impressed with their work.

"Night of the break-in, there were thunderstorms off and on all night," Lawrence said. "Didn't really amount to much, although the power was out till morning, but still . . . the thief gets all the way into a property with a long driveway and gets up to the second floor, where there are two people. Adults. I mean . . . you have to believe there's some clue to find, don't you? But these sheriff department guys? Nothing."

The reason Immigration had become involved, Lawrence explained—Freddy had wondered about that—was that the thief had apparently scooped a pair of passports with the other loot. Normally not a big deal, but it was in this case because the guests who lost the passports were from Moldova. Freddy wanted to know if that was in Pennsylvania or maybe Iowa, so Lawrence didn't say anything more until they arrived at Bedside Manor. There, the silence was not so much broken as shattered, for the two young owners had a peculiar habit of doubling up everything, no matter which of them spoke first.

"They were in the Mill Room, the two guests," the woman explained. "It's our most popular suite because of the water wheel and the great view."

To which her husband echoed, "Yeah, the view from the Mill Room is great. And it has the water wheel. It's our most popular room." He added, "It's booked solid all season. A new couple coming in tonight."

"Yes, a new couple tonight. Every night is sold out," his wife put in. "Booked right into November."

"The middle of November," the husband said.

Before any further refinements could be inserted, Freddy quickly put in his wish to see the room where the burglary had taken place. The wish was granted with a surprising absence of chatter, so that the impact of the Mill Room struck him full on, right at the doorway. For a guy whose living experience was exclusively tenth floor and above, in glass and concrete, the Mill Room was almost an adventure—so much so that at first he didn't even notice the grinding noise from the old wooden gears on the level below.

For a long time, Freddy didn't move from the doorway, but simply stood and stared at the opposite wall, where a pair of windows offered a close-up view of the water wheel turning slowly outside. He was more fascinated by the wheel than he would ever admit to anyone, and allowed himself to enjoy the hypnotic effect of its paddles rising across the bottom half of the right window, then reappearing in the left on their way back down to the stream below. Although he didn't have the inclination to express the thought—much less the vocabulary—Freddy was struck by the timelessness of the water wheel. There was something so huge and relentless, yet gentle about it.

His reverie was broken by a matched set of comments from behind.

"The best view is to your right."

"Yes, view to your right. Through the picture window."

"The wall with the picture window."

Freddy held his hand out behind him, palm out. He meant it to keep the others from following him into the room, for he always liked to get the feel of a scene with no one else around, but it had the effect of silencing the voluble young owners. They hadn't exaggerated the beauty of the view, however. Craggy, maple-covered hills spread from one end of the horizon to the other, split here and there by small farms. From a V-shaped cleft in the limestone he could see the beginning of the gentle stream that flowed down toward them and on under the mill. The scene had a kind of peace that was entirely foreign to him.

With more than a little reluctance, Freddy turned to the details of the room. He noted the table opposite the king-sized bed, where the guests had put their money and jewelry—and passports.

"Didn't hear a thing, the two of them told me," Lawrence had come into the room and now stood beside Freddy. "The noise from the water wheel—well, not so much the wheel itself, but it turns the gears. You can hear them below."

"We run it pretty well all the time." The owners had followed Lawrence.

"All the time," came the echo. "Guests feel cheated if we don't."

"You have to do what the guests want. Besides it's kind of a soothing noise."

"Soothing."

For a moment, Freddy weighed the pleasures of the Mill Room against the possibility of more duplicated explanations from his tour guides and opted for leaving. He'd seen enough, anyway. And listened to more than he'd wanted to hear. Still, the Mill Room—the view, the setting, the atmosphere—it was something else. On the way back to his brother-in-law's place, it depressed him a bit when he realized that, if he told the guys in his precinct about the scam he'd uncovered here, they would not understand how nice a place the Bedside Manor might be to spend some time. They were all downtown guys just like him.

Freddy has uncovered what he believes to be a scam in the matter of the stolen passports (and money and jewelry). What has his investigation revealed?

WAS LAWRENCE REALLY THERE?

Marsha Thurman wasted no time getting to the point. "What I would like, Mr. Meeker," she said, placing a badly creased photograph on the counter, "what my firm would like, is for you to examine this photograph and then, if you believe it is authentic, to appear as an expert witness on behalf of our client, Lawrence Durban the Third. Naturally, we'll meet your per diem and expenses."

To a professional archivist, any photograph older than last week is irresistible, and Perry Meeker immediately began rotating his wheelchair left and right, a regular habit when something teased at his natural curiosity. The item in question was a standard-size black-and-white with the faded, sepia-like shading often seen in photos that have aged in an attic or dresser drawer. It offered an everyday small town scene: three men, two of them older than the third, standing on a sidewalk on what must have been the main street. To the left of the two older men, the camera had caught the elbow of a bystander, pretty much establishing that whoever took the picture was not a professional. On their right, the two were almost but not quite covered by a large awning that hung over the sidewalk. Its front flap pronounced the store behind to be that of "Lawrence Durban, Dry Goods & Groceries."

"The two men standing together?" Marsha leaned across the counter. "The one holding up the umbrella is Lawrence Durban: Lawrence the First. The gentleman at his side with the fedora in his hand is Senator Grant. And under the awning? Just a bit behind them and to their right? The younger man? That's Lawrence Durban the Second, oldest son of . . . "

"Looks like he got into the picture by accident, doesn't it?" Perry interrupted. "Like maybe he'd just come out of the store and walked into the picture."

"Search me," Marsha replied, "but it doesn't matter why he's in it; the point is that he's in it. You see the litigation we're dealing with revolves around whether Lawrence number two there was actually alive the day this picture was supposedly taken. There's a date on the back in pencil."

Perry flipped the picture to confirm that fact while she continued. "August 15, '38. We have used the local newspaper archives to confirm that Senator Grant was definitely in town on that date, and since Lawrence Durban the First was something of a bagman for Grant's party, it's both logical and reasonable that the two would get together. And that they'd be photographed together."

Perry looked at her. "I've no doubt that by now you have cross-referenced to be sure the three men are indeed who they're supposed to be," he said. "Have you had the photograph examined to see if maybe it's been touched up?"

"Do you mean to see if Lawrence the Second was dubbed in electronically? Of course, first thing we did, but the results were equivocal. We had two experts go at it, and both agree that in the picture you're looking at, Lawrence number two was not added after the fact. But, and it's a big but, one expert says the picture could be a second generation."

Perry nodded. "I see. Someone could have dubbed him

into the original shot and then made a duplicate—the one I have here. In a duplicate, if it's done well enough, you can't tell there's been dubbing. Pretty clever." Perry set the photograph down and went back to rotating his wheelchair. "I think I have something for you, but first, why don't you satisfy my curiosity? What's the litigation all about?"

"Money, what else?" Marsha said. "Lawrence the Second was a bit of an odd duck, apparently. Not very reliable or businesslike. Certainly not a fusspot like the old man. More of a poet, I guess. Wasn't a good husband or father, either. It seems he had this habit of wandering off—would disappear for days at a time."

"Let me guess," Perry put in. "He was allegedly off on one of his disappearances on August 15, 1938, and nobody bothered to report it officially because he did this all the time. Right?"

"That's part of it," Marsha replied. "But it's more complicated than that. You see, on the evening of August 15, the date of the picture, the old man, Lawrence the First, was killed in a car accident. And—very uncharacteristic for him—he had no will. Since our province was one of the few in Canada at the time that still practiced a form of primogeniture—meaning the estate goes to the oldest son—it should have gone to Lawrence the Second. But about a week later good old Lawrence Two himself turned up among the dearly departed. His body was found in Cold Creek not far from town. That led to a tug of war in court for a couple of years over whether Lawrence Two was already dead before August 15. The judge found there was no evidence proving him alive, so the Durban money went to Lawrence Two's younger brother, Edward, because he was the oldest surviving son."

"Ah!" Perry was enjoying this. "But what this picture would do is show that number two Lawrence was very much alive on the fateful day and he—well, his descendants—should have got the cash!"

"Precisely!" Marsha, too, began to show enthusiasm. "And we have been retained by Lawrence Durban the Third to bring that about."

Perry let go of the wheelchair and picked up the picture once more. "It's too bad this is faked," he said. "It would have been such fun to be part of your case!"

"Fake? You mean it really is fake?"

"Oh, no question," Perry said. "That may well be the two Lawrences and Senator Grant there, and it may well be Durban's store, but there's no question this photo has been patched together from more than one source."

How does Perry know the photo has been "patched together"?

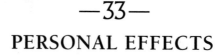

—33—
PERSONAL EFFECTS

"That's all? Just this box of clothes and a tote bag with ... what ... looks like a laptop and stuff?"

"Yeah, he had more clothes in his suite at the Plaza and some little rug thing, but that's already been sent over to the consulate. Apparently this guy was only in the country for about six weeks at a time, once a year, and he always stayed at the Plaza, so there was nothing but clothes and personal things."

"Then why didn't these clothes and the tote bag go to the consulate with the rest of it?"

"The clothes are the ones he was wearing when he shot himself. The lab had them till yesterday. I don't know about the tote bag."

"And now we get to fold and pack clothes that are all full of blood? Great! I always wanted to be a ghoul!"

"Don't be such a wuss! We got rubber gloves. Besides, it's . . . where's the calendar? One, two . . . it's four weeks ago today that it happened, so it's not like any of the blood is wet and smelly or anything."

"That's a real consolation."

"C'mon, it's not so bad. All we have to do is itemize everything, fold it like we really cared, and then take it to the Jordanian consulate, where we get somebody to sign for it."

"Well, if it's not so bad, then I nominate you as folder-in-charge-of-anything-with-blood-on-it! Especially under-wear. What's in the tote bag? Let's start with that."

"Why am I not surprised? Okay, I'll call out the items.

You write them on the inventory sheet, and then we'll switch and go through it all again to double-check."

"You done this before?"

"Yeah, once. They take this real seriously upstairs. Don't forget to date and time the sheet. May 25, and it's what? . . . 2:15 P.M."

"Now there's a coincidence!"

"What is?"

"This is a big day in Jordan. Their Independence Day."

"No kidding? Okay, here's the first . . . ooh, nice laptop! Looks like a . . . Hey, what's this? A rosary? That's weird. I thought everybody in Jordan was Muslim."

"There are lots of Christians in Jordan. Lemme see. Those are prayer beads, not a rosary! See? There's no crucifix and the . . . "

"How do you know so much about Muslims and Jordan?"

"I stayed awake in Mid-Eastern Studies. 'Kay, I'm writing down 'one set prayer beads.' Think I need to put the color or anything like that?"

"Nah . . . well, maybe. Just put down that they're brown. And then wait; we're gonna get mixed up. Let's finish the laptop. Okay, it's a Dell Inspiron 8000. Not bad! Serial's 482A-111X. Got all that? This is how he got the bad e-mail from his wife."

"What e-mail?"

"Seems he opened this e-mail the day before he shot himself. From his wife in Amman. Simply said, 'it has failed,' whatever 'it' is. Our guys notice it on the laptop, so they call the police in Amman and find out she's dead, too. Suicide. The same day she sent the message. Right away, then, our guys figure it's a pact. Something went wrong big time, so the two of them . . . boom!"

"Guy couldn't have been very religious then."

"Yeah, but he carried this rosary thing."

"I suppose so, but suicide is supposed to be a huge no-no for Muslims."

"Well, ours is not to reason why. And we're wasting time. Next up: celphone, Nokia 918. Better write 'cellular phone.' Two 'l's."

"I know. I stayed awake in spelling class."

"Good. Then spell meth . . . methylphen . . . "

"Methylphenidate?"

"Yeah, looks like that."

"Methylphenidate hydrochloride?"

"Yeah! How'd you know that?"

"That's Ritalin. It's a kid's drug, hyper kids. What's he doing with Ritalin?"

"Hey, don't ask me! Maybe he's got a kid like that. The bottle hasn't been opened. Here, see for yourself. '27/04/02, Third Avenue Pharmacy, Shareef Abu Ibrahim'—that's the dead guy's name."

"Could be his son's name, too."

"Doesn't make any difference to us. The rest of it says 90 meth . . . methylphen-whatever, 30 milligrams, 3 repeats, A.I. Jarash, M.D."

"Okay, okay, but I'm just putting down 'prescription drugs' and the pharmacy and date."

"Fine by me. Okay, next is the return half of an airline ticket. Royal Jordanian Airlines for May 2. First class."

"Might have guessed that! What else?"

"A PDA, Palm Pilot. Would I ever like to have one of these!"

"Wouldn't we all? That's everything then?"

"Yeah—no! I almost didn't see these down at the bottom. One pocket-sized memo pad and two ballpoint pens: Paper Mate Flexgrip. And that—just a minute—that, I am pleased to announce, is the last of it."

"Strange."

"Yeah, I know. He didn't seem the cheap pen type."

"I really wasn't thinking of the pens."

"What then?"

"The stuff in this tote bag makes me wonder if this guy really did commit suicide or if maybe he got offed."

"What makes you think that?"

Something in the tote bag makes one of the two speakers suspect that Shareef Abu Ibrahim may not have committed suicide. What is it?

—34—
THE RANKLED BROTHERS

The rays of early morning sun were weak, but the pale warmth felt comforting on the back of Kerry O'Brien's neck. Comforting and at the same time reassuring in a way that only those who endure long, cold winters can understand. This was the fourth clear day in a row following a heavy, late winter storm and Kerry, like everybody else in the county, was elated by the hope that spring might be on the way.

He drove up the long laneway with care. Just ahead was the spot where the deputy got stuck last night and needed a tow. The Rankin brothers—always referred to as the "Rankled Brothers" because of their legendary hatred for each other—were too old to plow out their lane and would never pay anyone to do it. Nothing unusual about that out here in the boonies, but the lane was a long one and a good storm could isolate the two of them for some time until a good-hearted neighbor finally brought a tractor and blower over to clear it out. It was one of those who had come in late yesterday afternoon and found Tommy dead in his kitchen beside the wood stove.

Kerry eased the coroner's official car past the ruts and banks created by the police car and tow truck and stopped for a minute to stare at the Rankins' house, amazed at what hate can do. Two identical one-story wings were butted together at the narrow ends and bisected by what may have been intended as a main entrance at one time, but was barely visible now behind the firewood stacked in front of it. The woodpile, carefully divided in two by a rusty sheet of corrugated tin, spread out in both directions, partly filling the long front porch.

Significant effort had gone into distinguishing the two halves of the house. The one on the left—Tommy's—had been painted a fire engine red that was now faded. Simon Rankin's half was a bright robin's egg blue. Tommy had put on shutters; Simon had not. Although both houses boasted flower boxes in the front windows, on Tommy's side one was broken; Simon's were newer and much larger. The roof of Simon's side, with its black asphalt shingles, was graced at the extreme north end by a weather vane. Tommy's roof, covered in snow, had no such ornament. Both sides had yellow brick chimneys of identical height and design, but, while Tommy's sported a rusted TV aerial, Simon had installed a satellite dish.

The Rankin "boys," only two years apart in age, had once been inseparable, but had fallen out over a racehorse they had inherited from their widower father. For Kerry, that event was lost in the mists of time: before medical school, before he had even finished high school, for he remembered the first time he had come up this lane as a teenager with a delivery from his father's store. The "Rankled Brothers" were already a local legend then. Now, after all these years of animosity, the two were finally parted once and for all.

"Looked like natural causes to me," was the opinion of the sheriff's deputy who'd gotten stuck yesterday. "No sign of violence I could see. Nothing on the body—well, nothing obvious. Anyway, you can see for yourself when you go down to Hammer's."

John Hammer was the local undertaker. Tommy's body was lying there waiting for Kerry to decide whether an autopsy was needed.

The door on Simon's end of the house opened just as Kerry lifted a fist to knock.

"What do you want?" Simon Rankin was a big man. He may have been old, but he filled the doorway with lusty strength. His voice did, too. "Well?" The old man was about to bluster further, but then cocked his head forward. "You . . . you're Tiff O'Brien's boy, aren't you? My God, you look like your mother. What are you doing here?"

"I'm the county coroner now, Mr. Rankin."

"The coroner! Young pup like you! Well, well. Your mother . . . she must be some proud. Guess you better come in."

Simon turned abruptly and left Kerry at the door. When he collected himself a few seconds later and followed the old man into the kitchen, Simon was jamming a stick of wood into the stove. In Kerry's opinion, it was already too hot in the room.

"Looks like she may get above freezing today, this sun stays up," Simon offered conversationally. "Be first time in a good long while." He wiped his hands on his trousers and plunked himself down in a rocking chair. Kerry stood awkwardly just inside the door.

"Sit down." The old man gestured vaguely at a chair by the kitchen table. "I suppose, you bein' the coroner, this is about Tommy. Well, I can't tell you anything. He's dead, the old fool, that's all I know. Haven't seen him in months, probably not since last fall. Didn't want to, neither. When I go out, I look first, and if he's there I stay in. He does the same, and that's just fine. Hear him, though—he's so darn noisy. Like the night before last, puttin' wood in the stove. And slammin' doors! Always did behave like he was born in the barn. His fault, you know, that thing with the horse. Suppose you know about that. Your mother probably told you. She'd understand, too."

Kerry listened to Simon for almost an hour, surprised at how voluble the old man was. Later, driving out the laneway, again using great care through the ruts, he wondered why he hadn't told Simon that his mother died last year. He wondered, too, just what it was that Simon thought his mother understood about the racehorse argument. He reached the road and turned toward town. By this time, he'd set aside thoughts of his mother and returned to what was making him uneasy. It was clear now he'd have to do an autopsy, for there was something about the case that did not make sense.

What is it that "did not make sense" to Kerry?

—35—
A CLEAR CASE OF ARSON

I should have known better. In this part of town, any car that looks even remotely official sticks out like a brass band, and on mine these big gold letters blare out ONTARIO FIRE MARSHALL on both front doors. Not that anybody would throw rocks or anything. After all it was daytime and, even if the neighborhood is pretty seedy, this is Toronto, not . . . well, L.A. or Liverpool. Or Belfast. Oh, we got our share of bad stuff. Trust me, we do, but . . . Sorry, I'm getting sidetracked. What I mean by "should have known better" is that, if you show up in the streets around here looking like you're connected with authority, all you get is a freeze. Nobody knows anything; nobody's seen anything. But then, you can't blame the people, really. Cop cars, city cars—and cars from the Fire Marshall's office—they never show up here just to do PR.

Anyway, here's the reason for my brain cramp. Simple enough, really. See, what I was planning to do was make a quick detour to our office off Lakeshore Road and pick up one of the unmarked Hyundais, but Emma Leo called me on my cell with the lab results on the bicycle tracks. What Emma had for me was . . . oh, I guess I should first tell you that I was investigating a fire. There's this kind of . . . well, gazebo, I guess you could call it, in Serena Gundy Park. Belongs to the city, and it's pretty popular for weddings and things like that in the summer. A bit of lawn around it and lots of trees. Serena Gundy's in a valley, and when you're at the gazebo you're completely isolated from the city. Nice spot. Well . . . it was until somebody torched the gazebo last week.

No question it was arson, and amateur at that. The torch used so much kerosene, you could smell it before you even got to the scene. We'd have been called in anyway—the Fire Marshall's office, I mean. It's mandatory if there's a blaze in a public building. Anyway, the file landed on my desk, which is kind of coincidental, because I live near the park and actually saw the fire—well, the smoke, really—from my apartment balcony. That's not important, though. Just thought I'd mention it. Doesn't often happen.

Okay, Emma's phone call. See, there's bike trails all through the park, a few of them asphalt, but most are them are left natural. There's one of these goes right by the gazebo. Here's where we had a bit of, well . . . not luck, really . . . smart thinking, I suppose you'd call it. The fire captain on the first truck in, he made a sharp call. The gazebo was fully involved by the time they got there—couldn't possibly have been saved—and, of course, he smells the kerosene, so he holds back the crew. Then he spots this single set of bike tracks, so they were blocked and preserved before things got hosed down. We got good impressions because there's a lot of clay in the soil there.

Now like I said, I was in my official car heading for Lakeshore when Emma called me on my cell. This part had to be straight luck—that she called right when she did. You'll see what I mean in a minute.

"They're Dunlops, those tires," Emma says. "And we may have caught a bit of a break. These tires were a special production for a mountain bike called Phrygia. Made in Italy for Wal-Mart."

Of course, immediately I want to know why this is such

a break for us, and Emma tells me that, although these bikes were produced exclusively for Wal-Mart, they were sold only in the States.

"According to the Wal-Mart guy," she says, "none of these bikes ever made it to a Canadian Wal-Mart store."

And I reply, "So what's to keep anybody in Toronto from buying one of these Phrygias in Buffalo?"

"Why would they?" Emma says. "There was nothing all that special about them. And even if some bikes got here via Buffalo, or Detroit, or Niagara Falls, or wherever, there's got to be only a few of them."

I'm about to argue with that, when I realize I've gone past the exit to Lakeshore—this is why I ended up making the call in my official car—but the pause gives Emma just enough time to get off on another tack.

"Both tires, front and back, are the same tread design," she puts in. "Not always the case with mountain bikes. And one of the tracks—it's 47 millimeters wide, by the way—the track that weaves a bit—I think this tire may have different mileage on it from its partner. Does that help you at all? Tread's four millimeters deep on average, while the partner track is 53 wide and six deep. Looks like one tire could have had more use. And there's more!"

Emma is thorough, but she darn near kills you with information.

"A couple of grooves in the treads of both tires seem to have picked up something. I'm 95 percent positive they're small stones, so almost for sure your bike rider had to be on a path with grit-type gravel before going near the gazebo."

We went back and forth a couple more times, and she

was starting to say the same stuff all over again, so I told her she was breaking up, but by this time I had passed two more exits and was coming up on the Dufferin Gate so, official car or not, I just kept going.

Now here's the luck part—Emma calling me when she did, I mean—and also the part about knowing better. See, I went to the neighborhood to talk to these two teenagers, Gilroy and Ferguson Sills. They're brothers, both have quite a juvy sheet, and both had been seen at a gas station beside Serena Gundy Park not long before the fire—with mountain bikes! They had been filling their tires at the air pump and eventually had been shooed away by the owner for disturbing other customers.

I had just made the turn onto Atlanta Avenue, where the Sills live, when I spotted this skinny little kid shooting hoops. One of the Sills, or else the pictures on my passenger seat were lying to me. Another break, 'cause I had not wanted to question the boys together. The kid didn't turn until I got out of the car and slammed the door. Then one look at the lettering on the door, and you could see the ice slide over his face.

There was a mountain bike leaning against the chainlink fence to one side of the basket. The bike was Easter-egg purple, and in bright yellow along the crossbar I could read "Phrygia" plain as day.

I tried an opening sally: "Nice bike."

He shrugged, and then looked at me for the longest time, no expression at all on his face. Then he turned and dropped a three-pointer right from where he stood. The ball swished through and bounced up and down below the basket. He watched until it settled down and then slowly walked over and sat on it, almost—but not quite—facing me.

"My brother's," he said finally.

I'd almost forgotten what I'd said to him! I tried, "Good shot," nodding at the basket.

That got another shrug.

"Your brother a hoop man, too?"

Shrug.

"How come he's not playing with you? Bit of one-on-one?"

The shoulders came up, but then held. "Football," he said finally after a long pause, and the shoulders fell.

"Your brother's playing football?"

Nod. Just a small one. Then in his eyes I noticed what in anyone else I might have called a spark of pride. In this kid, I wasn't too sure. "Rams," he said. "Street tryouts today."

The Rams are a junior football team with a pretty big reputation around here. Every spring the coaches set aside a couple days for off-the-street tryouts on the outside chance there just might be a discovery.

"Looking for Mercury Street," I said. "Right around here, isn't it?" That was completely spur of the moment. I had no idea whether he'd buy it or not, but playing lost was all I could think of to make him think my stopping here was just an everyday thing. See, by then I knew that, if either of these brothers was riding near that gazebo on a Phrygia mountain bike, for sure it had to be the other one. I didn't want the one I was talking with to think I was on to something.

Why is the fire investigator sure that if either of the brothers rode near the gazebo on the day of the fire, it is the other one, not the one she is speaking to?

THE IRISH PROBLEM

Anno Domini MDCCCXXXIX
SEPTIMUS IUNIUS

To the Colonial Secretary,

His Excellency Baron Walpole of Henley, Greetings

Regrettably, I must beg leave to report yet another incident arising from what is commonly referred to as "the Irish Problem" in Her Majesty's colony of Upper Canada. Whilst the trouble among the Irish manifests itself throughout the colony, there is particularly strong conflict between the Protestant smithies and shopkeepers in the village of Killarney and Catholic farmers in the settlement tract known as Mount St. Patrick. The incident to which I refer hereto is the burning of the Loyal Orange Lodge in Killarney on the twenty-eighth of March last.

The fire was deliberately set and, although it could not be so, blame has been laid on Papists from Mount St. Patrick. I fear that the desire of the residents of Killarney for vengeance may lead to violence, which, in turn, is sure to provoke a compensating response from the Papists. Fortunately, the distance between Mount St. Patrick and Killarney requires some effort to traverse. There being no roads, the only reasonable means is by barge on a canal of some twenty leagues, which leads from the Catholic area to the Shan River. There is then an additional leg of travel by river (five leagues) between the mouth of the canal and Killarney. In winter, this route is too treacherous to undertake, and to go through the bush is impossible. During the growing season, I have observed that all the colonists are too filled with the need to ensure a good harvest to risk leaving their homes.

As a consequence, the Irish Problem asserts itself only twice a year. In the spring, trouble occurs between what the colonists call "spring break-up" and planting time. (The lodge, for example, was burned two days after the ice broke up and flowed out of the Shan River.) In autumn, the trouble resumes after the harvest is in and continues until what is called here, "freeze-up."

Therefore, I beg Your Excellency's leave to request that Her Majesty's Fourth Regiment of Foot be ordered to remain at its current posting until the arrival of replacements next summer. The presence of troops here, especially during the upcoming period between the completion of the harvest and the onset of winter, is in my humble opinion the only way to keep peace between the Protestant and the Catholic Irish.

With respect, I remain Your humble servant,

> Diogenes Simpson
> Justice of the Peace for the Nelson District,
> Her Majesty's Colony of Upper Canada
> God Save the Queen

Diogenes Simpson reports that the Papists from the Mount St. Patrick settlement tract are being blamed for the deliberate burning of the Loyal Orange Lodge in Killarney "although it could not be so." Why could they not have done it?

—37—
CHOOSING THE RIGHT CLIENT

The people who hired him he called "customers." The people he shot he called "clients." It was only one of his many eccentricities. Another was using a Ross rifle for takedowns. It was an old weapon, almost an antique, and had a well-deserved reputation for jamming when it got hot. Canadian soldiers had brought the Ross to World War I, and to a man they threw it away as soon as they could scoop up something else. The jamming didn't concern him, for he never fired more than a single shot. Nor did other drawbacks, such as the exceptionally long barrel and the weird shell ejection system, for the Ross, whatever its faults, was unfailingly accurate and, in his line of work, accuracy was pretty much all that mattered.

He often wondered what it would be like to get into a discussion about the merits of this rifle, or about the scope he'd taken off a Browning and modified, something else he knew was eccentric. But in his business they didn't hold conventions, and there were no newsletters. It was a faceless, nameless world he worked in, where nods and gestures and grunts were substitutes for conversation, and where—he found this very amusing—his customers referred to an assignment as a contract, although no signature, nor even a handshake, would ever be part of it.

At the moment the Ross was pointed across a city street. Sometime in the next minute or so he was going to fire it. That much was for sure. He'd taken money from a customer and he'd carry through; he always did. There was some uncertainty in the situation though, and it had made him uneasy for a short while. Somebody else in the business might have packed up and moved out. Got more information, a better description of the client. But not him, for he appreciated—even enjoyed—the uncertainty of this situation, and the challenge.

The customer in this case, like most of them, had made every effort to be anonymous and, also like most, had given no names, provided no pictures. In fact, he'd offered as little information as he possibly could, for information left a potential trail. They'd met after dark the previous night in a flat-rate parking lot outside a sports coliseum. The game inside had started an hour before.

"He's average weight and average height, this guy, but he's got a full moustache," the customer had said from the back seat. "And he's completely bald. Both arms covered with tattoos, those cheap, makeshift ones you get in prison. Got a bit of that stoop guys get from doing a lot of time in max. I gather you know something about what that's like?"

Customers invariably brought up his jail time if they knew about it, but he never reacted.

The customer kept talking. "He broke out of Stony Mountain three weeks ago, and I know for a fact the cops are closing in, so there's no time to fool around. There's $10,000 in that bag beside me. Down payment. The rest you get after you do it. Tomorrow! There's a flower shop on the west side of Bay, just north of College. I'm not sure of the exact number, but it's in the low 800s. He'll be picking up a package there some time between 11:00 A.M. and noon. Get him then. It'll be the only opportunity."

With that, the customer had slipped out of the back seat and disappeared into the night, leaving the bag of cash as promised. Also as promised, however vaguely, at 11:05 A.M. this morning the client had appeared at the door of Love 'n' Roses, 810 Bay Street. He'd stopped on the sidewalk, taken a card from his pocket and appeared to confirm the name and address, then stepped to the door, where he stood motionless for several long seconds before finally pulling it open and going in.

All this was carefully observed from across the street through the target circle of the modified scope. It had a black site post instead of a bull's eye, a change that permitted a wider and clearer view of a client's immediate surroundings. Without it he could still have discerned average height and average weight, but the scope made it clear the man had a moustache. It would likely have shown the tattoos as well, except that the client's arms were fully covered. His head, too. Rain had been falling since dawn. Not a hard rainfall, but just enough, and with enough wind to make someone opt for a jacket and hood. Nevertheless, with or without the confirming tattoos and bald head, he'd have taken out the client when he paused before the door had it not been for another man who, at precisely that moment, passed Love 'n' Roses on his way to Cecily Mae's Gift Shoppe.

He had noticed Cecily Mae's when he arrived. It was at 822 Bay, and the sidewalk in front of it was loaded with cut flowers for sale. The scope told him there were more inside. This alternate client—the one who went into Mae's—was also average-average. He had a moustache, and there was no question he was bald. He wore a jacket but no hat, and he, too, had stopped on the sidewalk and appeared to check the store's address against a card. Like the client at Love 'n' Roses, this one had a bit of a stoop, but then, because of the rain, so did everyone else on the street. After a glance behind him over his left shoulder, the alternate client had turned abruptly and walked into Mae's.

Two targets. But only one of them was the real client. He moved his shoulders a degree or two. That was all it took to shift the muzzle of the old Ross from Cecily Mae's to Love 'n' Roses. He shifted back and forth between the stores several times, before making his final decision. Then he took a deep breath and let it out slowly. Both men would be exiting soon. He was ready.

On what basis has he chosen the client?

SOMEWHERE IN THE DESERT

POLICE HELP!
Two men —black chevy pickup —
Reds tied on floor behind seat —hairy guy
pushing head down —hand smells pickle?
Coughs a lot —big. Driver no info
Drove round and round —many bumps then
straight on pavement. 10 min? then dirt 30?
Now in desert Treat OK
NB blanket covering me had hole at waist
Spot of sunlight to right when pavement —
to feet when dirt —don'

Sapphire   Kitty Leaman   Goldie   Jake   HELP!

"How we know this here note ain't fake?" asked the burly
man in faded jeans and a rumpled brown shirt that said "Lobo
County Deputy Sheriff" at each shoulder. "Fishy enough some
trucker finds it and brings it in." He poked a grimy finger at
his Smokey hat on the table in front of him.

The other, somewhat younger man in the tiny room had a
similar shirt, but wore trousers to match. His hat hung on a
wall peg above him. He tapped the note when he answered.

"Because Sapphire and Goldie . . . the third one's got to say
'Jake' . . . they were Kitty's goldfish when she was little. Smart
kid to put that in."

"Yeah, but the trucker . . . "

"Look, Corlin. With that windstorm late yesterday, this note
could easily be somewhere in Mexico. I'd say we're just lucky.

The kid, too, that we got it, but like I say she's smart. Don't know how she did it, but just getting a note out into that wind was—"

There was a quick tap on the door before it opened. A woman chewing ferociously on a stick of gum stepped in and pointed at the fully uniformed man. "Helicopter's here in ten minutes, Tom. And there's four FBI types comin' in, not two. They said they want to pick you up and head right out for the . . . for the . . . 'most likely search area,' they called it."

The deputy in jeans sat back in his chair, transparent relief on his face that it was not he who had to select the most likely search area. Tom, on the other hand, appeared to have other items on his mind.

"Did you hear from Red yet? Whether he got hold of . . . what's her name, again, Theresa? The waitress?"

The crackle and pop of the gum stopped abruptly. "Sorry," the woman answered. "Just so much going on, I almost . . . " She dug into the pocket of her blouse and produced a slip of paper. "Theresa's off at her sister's in Coyne. Here's the number, so you can talk to her yourself if you want. Says she remembers serving the kid yesterday 'bout halfway through the breakfast special. Red says that'd be 'bout nine. Didn't see any two big men. She'd remember, too, Theresa would. I can tell you that."

Tom ran his left hand along his chin and spoke very deliberately. "Next time, Emma Jean, give me that kind of information immediately."

The gum took a beating as Tom continued. "Now you drop whatever you're doing and go take Corlin's cruiser down to the fairgrounds and pick up those FBI folks when the helicopter lands. Bring them here and we'll have the 'most likely search area' set out for them."

Corlin almost snorted. "How ya gonna do that?" he wanted to know. "We got no witnesses. Nobody saw no black Chevy pickup and nobody saw two guys like this here note says, neither!"

"She's pretty much told us where to look, Corlin," Tom replied. "The note's got enough—"

This time Corlin did snort. "Yeah, sure! So they go round and round and go over bumps."

Tom continued to be almost serenely patient. "That can only mean they went in and out of a couple of parking lots down by Red's. Either they were trying to confuse her—which I hope—or else they were lost themselves—which I hope not."

"How come?"

"Because if they're trying to confuse her, they plan to keep her alive. If they were confused themselves, then they have no plan, and heaven knows what they might do. But that doesn't matter for the moment. We've got enough to narrow the search."

Corlin was still dubious, but was more respectful now. "The pavement?" he asked. "And the dirt roads? There's only four roads outta town and every one a' them's paved. Once they're outta town and out in the desert, there ain't nothin' but dirt roads leadin' off a' every one a' them."

"Read the note again, Corlin. It points to the most likely search area."

What information in the note, combined with what the two officers know, points to the most likely search area?

—39—
J.T.C. KAPCHEK'S
OPENING LECTURE

F irst-year students choosing Basic Medical Forensics
171 invariably made two incorrect assumptions when
they signed up for the course. One was that it was a "bird
course," because the syllabus described it simply as "a
basic overview of crime scene investigation." The other was
that, given the name J.T.C. Kapchek, the instructor must
be male. Also invariably, both mistakes were corrected in
the initial seconds of the opening lecture.

Striding into the crowded lecture hall, Dr. Kapchek
pointed to a pair of television screens and instantly caught
the room's attention with her booming voice.

"I want you to focus on one of the two screens on either
side of the chalkboard." The instruction carried effortlessly
to the back of the room. "You are about to assess the work
of a pair of investigators at the scene of a crime." She
tipped her head forward and peered over her glasses with
an expression that conveyed her suspicion that the task
might be too deep for some of them.

"They fail to do something—possibly a subtle error in
the minds of some, but a mistake nevertheless because
they do not use their heads. Now we're going to see if you
can use yours. You may have earned the marks to qualify
for admission to these hallowed halls, but all that means is
you have a good memory. Any damn fool with stamina
and a memory can pull the grades necessary to get in
here. What I want to know is: do you deserve to stay?
Watch the screen." She looked over her glasses again.

The students would soon discover this was a regular habit.

"By the way," she added. "This is Basic Medical Forensics 171. For the half of you that will drop the course after this class, I just want you to be sure you're in the right place. For the moment."

She waited for the buzz to die down. It did, quickly. "To give you some context before we begin: the victim in this scene has been murdered. Ritually, it would appear, or at least, in a manner that makes it clear this is not a random killing. You'll see what I mean in a few seconds. The other thing you need to know is that this is the fourth such murder in a period of ten weeks. They have probably all been committed by the same person, but authorities are nowhere near an arrest or even naming a suspect. Thus, circumstantial evidence, and keeping track of that evidence, becomes absolutely crucial. The investigation of this scene requires extreme care, precaution, and diligence. I will show you a portion of it, and you will tell me the mistake that you see."

J.T.C. Kapchek leaned toward the control panel and then paused. "By the way, you do not require any crime scene expertise for this. Just thoughtfulness."

As soon as the screens came into proper focus, the ritual or "message" aspect of the murder was obvious. The body of a slim adult male lay face down in a pool of blood that spread from both sides of his upper torso across a gray-tiled floor. From the top of the victim's head protruded the handle of a dagger. The handle was ornate, and more or less parallel to the floor. Very little fluid appeared around the point of penetration, suggesting that the dagger had been pushed in after the victim was dead.

The lighting was arranged so that, in the video, the walls of the room were pretty much in darkness. Even when the camera moved to show two investigators, clad in plastic coveralls with shoe coverings, surgical gloves and shower caps, it revealed nothing else in the room, aside from a small table. On the table sat an open satchel and, beside it, several extra pairs of surgical gloves, a pair of cameras, measuring tape, plastic evidence bags, a notebook and pen, a can of spray paint, and a pocket folder with several tweezers and other small implements.

First, the investigators measured the extent of the blood flow on either side of the body, recorded the time the measurements were taken, and then carefully pho-tographed the victim from several angles. Next, one of them put on a surgical mask and bent very close to the body, examining it slowly and carefully. At one point he stopped and, using tweezers, lifted something from the victim's shirt and put it in an evidence bag. The other investigator then put plastic bags over the victim's hands and feet and very carefully raised the victim's head while the other pulled a protective bag over it and the dagger. One investigator next scooped samples of the blood from different places into separate evidence bags, while his partner rolled out a plastic sheet parallel to the body, being careful not to let it touch the blood.

The first investigator put on a fresh pair of gloves, while the second one spray-painted an outline of the body. The two then stood at either end of the victim, crossed their arms at the elbows, and with one grabbing the shoulders, the other the ankles, raised the victim and laid him face up on the adjacent sheet.

Dr. Kapchek leaned toward the control panel, keeping a watchful eye on the nearest screen. She waited while the first investigator took off his gloves again, retrieved a camera, and took photographs of the outline. When his partner bent over to begin a close-up examination of the front of the body, Kapchek hit the Off switch.

"That's enough," she said above the low stir that buzzed through the room. "By now you have seen what they failed to do."

What is the failure?

—40—

THE CHAIN OF THE PEOPLE

The boys sat in Lotus position, side by side in a semi-circle, with arms linked. One or two were naked, but most wore loose, brown loincloths. All of them wore sandals made of tree bark and strangler vine. The old man in front of them, his back to the setting sun, was also in lotus position but had no use for sandals: the soles of his feet were covered in calluses thicker than any bark could match. He too wore a loincloth, but it was pulled under his crotch and fastened at the back like a diaper. A set of thick, ropy scars ran parallel down one cheek and disappeared beneath his wild gray beard before resurfacing on his chest. If he had once had a name, it was long forgotten. To all the clans he was known only as "Storyteller."

The boys in front of him were unusually attentive for young adolescents. In part that was because of the respect the old man commanded, but mostly they were just eager to hear the rest of the story of the Chain of the People. They could see this legendary talisman hanging around Storyteller's neck, the visible part resting atop his long beard. One of his hands continually stroked its surface, an index finger occasionally looping around the inside of the links. These—there were twenty altogether—were just a bit bigger than the old man's dark eyes and appeared to be gold, but might have been bronze or some other alloy.

Metal was rare among the people, and most of the boys stared fixedly at the chain, but some, especially the younger ones, could not take their gaze away from Storyteller's hand. His fingers were extraordinarily long, and seemed exceptionally straight and powerful for one so ancient, but his thumb hung without bone or muscle support and flopped about with every movement.

"The Chain of the People," Storyteller said for the fourth time in as many minutes, but this time added, "Tonight you see it for the first time. When you become a true hunter, when you have made your first kill and bring food home to the people, then you will be allowed to touch it, too."

He lapsed into silence as he stroked the chain. The boys waited. "It is complete, the chain," he said finally, "like our people, each link joined to the next."

The stroking continued.

"It was not always so."

Another long pause.

"Once, the five clans were enemies, each one jealous of the others. There was no comfort around the night fires, and in the day there was killing." Storyteller put four long fingers through adjacent links and pushed them forward. "The chain was divided. Each clan held an equal part, and each craved the parts of the others."

Several of the boys began to fidget. They had heard this the night before: how the chain was broken into parts, and how all the clans knew in their hearts they would have peace only if the chain were joined into one piece with no beginning and no end. Before he'd fallen asleep right in front of them, Storyteller had told them how the elders had tried to bring this about, how they had learned that far away by the Great Water were artisans with the skill to open links and join them together. But to open even one link and close it around another, these artisans demanded the skin of a white cirra as payment.

"Until Binwar," Storyteller had told the boys, "mighty Binwar, no hunter, and not even a whole clan, had ever taken more than two white cirra in a lifetime. And to join all five pieces of chain, to pay the artisans to make the chain whole, the elders understood they would need five! Five white cirra!"

The fidgeting stopped as Storyteller brought his good hand out from behind his beard and splayed thumb and fingers wide, then made a fist. "Binwar made it possible for the clans to be one people, for it was he who brought five white cirra to the council fires . . . five!" He paused again, but the boys were totally absorbed now. None of them had ever seen a cirra, white or otherwise, and weren't even sure what one would look like, but if Storyteller said the cirra was real, then it must be so. Besides, Binwar was the greatest hunter their people had ever known; if there were five white cirra to be found here in the mountains, surely he, of all the people, would have found them.

Storyteller continued: "At the council fires there was great excitement. Never before had the elders known such an opportunity, and they all quickly agreed that Binwar should make the journey to the artisans by the Great Water. All but Kor."

The mention of Kor made the boys stir, for in every one of the people's legends he was the arch-villain.

"Kor refused to give up his clan's portion of the Chain until the rest of the elders agreed that he would make the journey too. No one wanted this, for wherever Kor went trouble followed. But the elders had spoken."

With great deliberateness, Storyteller turned toward the setting sun. Darkness was falling swiftly. When he turned back to the boys, his eyes were half closed and his voice became softer. "It was on the night of the day they reached the Great Water that Kor disappeared. And so did one white cirra skin. But on the next day . . . "

The old man's head slumped forward for a moment, making the chain jangle slightly. The noise seemed to bring him back. "On the next day, Binwar went to the artisans with the five pieces of chain from each clan and with the four remaining skins . . . "

The boys watched Storyteller's aged face slide raggedly into a smile, lips after cheeks, and then eyes after lips. ". . . to make the Chain of the People whole."

With that, the sun dropped below the horizon. The old man's head dropped, too, and the boys knew they had heard all they were going to on this night. The mystery of how Binwar got the artisans to accept only four white cirra skins to turn the five pieces of chain into one continuous loop would have to wait until tomorrow night.

Five-Minute Mysteries *readers, however, can't wait. How did Binwar get the artisans to do it?*

SOLUTIONS

1. SAFETY INSPECTION

How does the WSB inspector know this?

When the WSB inspector sat in her car observing the construction site—particularly the two-by-four safety rail Sully had allegedly put up around the third-floor ledge—she noted that the nail heads used to install the rail were gleaming back at her in the sunlight. If the railing had been put up four weeks before, and was untouched (except by rain) because of the strike, even galvanized nail heads would not be gleaming by this time. They would be rusted or at least oxidized. The inspector quite rightly suspects that this is a very recent installation, probably one that took place after Sully's death.

2. THE BEST-LAID PLANS . . .

What was Linc Dennebar's one big mistake?

Linc wore gloves throughout the affair so he wouldn't leave fingerprints. That means, however, that his prints are not on Mary's telephone, which he used to report the crime.

3. RECOVERY AT DUSK

Stan Livy has become aware that something is not as it should be, and therefore calls off the operation. What is the "hitch" he discovers?

The new member of the team had provided accurate information so far. When she described the security system, she said there were motion-response cameras on top of the wall. Stan suspects a possible trap, or at least a "hitch," because, if the cameras respond to motion, the one above the gate where he is posted should have followed the old man on the pony. Instead, it is pointing across the valley. Stan must wonder what else is not as it should be.

4. CLOSING IN ON THE HACKER

Why does Tara Kiniski believe this is not the hacker the ICS team must catch?

Tara is aware that hackers spend ten to twelve hours a day or more at keyboards, seven days a week. With that kind of activity, it does not take very long for calluses to form on the fingertips. A true hacker, therefore, will not yield a set of perfect fingerprints. (Except for the thumbs, which are not used for keyboarding; for that reason both hackers and "civilians" produce clear thumbprints.)

5. A SAFE SHELTER?

Tyl has decided there is no one in the mill. What has led him to this conclusion?

Tyl noted that pigeons had made a home in the ruined mill. If the problem of starvation is bad enough for people to be eating rats, it's a certainty that anyone occupying the ruined mill will have caught and eaten the pigeons.

6. MULE TRAIN

Major Morton knows there is something that would certainly have alerted the trooper to the passing of the mule train had he been alert and at his post. What is that?

Any herd of animals fairly close together in warm conditions, especially if they are and have been active, will emit a level of odor that is impossible to miss. Twenty to twenty-five working mules, in summer warmth, in the relative confinement of a ravine would certainly smell, and, since there was "only a bit of wind" according to Hampton, the odor would not have been carried away. Trooper Hampton is either a heavy sleeper or, as Major Morton suspects, he wandered away from his post or took a bribe to let the train go through.

7. WHY GRANNY DOESN'T RETIRE

Why is Alice convinced that Torrey Mackilroy has talked to Pauline Ortona recently?

Torrey and Pauline were very close friends in high school, close enough to warrant quite an amount of comment in the yearbook biographies. Alice is struck by the fact that despite such an intense friendship, Torrey is not the least bit curious when approached by a private investigator. She doesn't ask what has gone wrong, why Polly is missing, how she is, what she'd done, etc.—all natural questions one might expect. The only reason for that, Alice surmises, is that Torrey already knows the answers.

8. TRANSCRIPT: CROWN VS. JERGENS

What is the "error" in Kaster's testimony to which the judge refers?

No matter what the county, or even the hemisphere, when a full moon first appears over the horizon, it never does so in the west. Kaster may think he saw the tractor silhouetted against the moon, but before the ten o'clock news on an August night it could not have happened that way if his porch is on the west side of his house.

9. "ODD BILLY" AND THE BACKPACK

What is the flaw in Billy's explanation of how he found the backpack?

Billy said he smelled smoke yesterday when he was on the logging road, went to investigate the campsite a couple of hundred yards away, and found the backpack. But there is no way he would have been able to smell smoke from the road that day.

Since the morning sun was in Sharnell's face when they were in the car, she was driving east. At Billy's instruction, she turned right (south) and drove down the straight logging road for about three minutes. Billy pointed out her side window (to the east) and told her it was at this point that he had smelled smoke.

The weather person on the radio said that the day's weather would be a repeat of the previous day's, with a stiff breeze from the west-southwest. Such a breeze would blow the smell of smoke away from the logging road, not toward it. From two hundred yards away, Billy could not have smelled a smoldering campfire.

10. THE IDENTIKIT DECISION

What evidence suggests to Wally that the moustache was a fake?
The crime scene investigator describes the liquor bottle as having a trace of some kind of adhesive around the rim. It is not only possible but likely that it came from a moustache that was glued on.

11. WAITING FOR SAHDEEN

What did the van driver do that was so stupid?
The gray Ford Windstar turned the wrong way onto a one-way street. A terrorist who is trying to keep a low profile,

who is being looked for, and who knows the city well would not make such a mistake. Max is behind the wheel and has pulled in his elbow because a jogger on the sidewalk bumped it. Harry is watching cyclists and cars in the side mirror from the passenger seat. Therefore, the van is parked on the left side of the street. Since a stakeout team would not draw attention to itself by parking illegally, the street must be a one-way. When the Windstar exited Old Church Towers (which they could see through the windshield), it turned toward them, because Harry told Max to get the licence plate number as it came close. The Windstar was going the wrong way, something sure to attract attention.

12. JUST A DEAD BATTERY

What leads Lily diSantos to the idea that the diplomatic issue is probably a distraction?

The dog walker found the note and jeweler's case outside in the alley behind the Eckmans' street at first light this morning. But rain had fallen after the robbery, for the patrol car returning from the site had its windshield wipers on. The note would not have been pristine and creamy smooth if raindrops had fallen on it. Someone is attempting to make it appear that the robbery has political motives, thereby adding a distraction to the investigation.

13. AN EXCERPT FROM SCENE THREE

Which one is a prime suspect, and on what basis does Curtis make that claim?

All three suspects would have knowledge of the balcony off the bedroom, and can be expected to have sufficient knowledge of the ravine to negotiate it in the dark – and it is very dark: no moon, no stars, no streetlight. But only the son, Roly, would know on which side of the bed Joe Beingessner sleeps. Since the shooting is premeditated, only Roly would know where to place the shots without any light to guide him.

14. THE NEW DEPUTY TAKES A WRONG STEP

How does Tim know the electrified fence system is not working properly?

Tim noted that grass and weeds have grown up under the electrified fence, high enough to hide it in some places. He does not need to have rural experience to know that this would ground the charge. The transformer may indeed be sending out a jolt every three seconds, but grass that touches the wire, especially wet grass from the shower last night, will simply conduct the jolt into the ground, rendering the fence ineffective. Any animal will yield to the temptation of better, or different, food on the other side of a low wire, cows being a notorious example. (What Tim may or may not know, but could soon find out from his rural colleagues, is that cows have deeply rooted follow-the-leader behavior. Once one goes through a failed fence, others will follow quickly.)

15. TAGGERT'S TURF

Why does Simpson Taggert disagree with the "involuntary" element in the killing of Mr. Banjee?

In the early morning, Simpson Taggert turns south on Fawcett Avenue. He pauses at 20 Fawcett to look at the fibrous begonias, which thrive on morning sun. Number 20 and all even numbered properties, therefore, must be on the west side of the street, which puts odd-numbered properties like number 41, the Banjee house, on the east side. In the early morning at the front of her house, therefore, Mrs. Banjee would not be suddenly surprised by a shadow, for the entire front would be in shadow. After noon, when the sun has moved into the south and toward the west, a shadow could be cast by someone approaching her porch, but not until then.

Mrs. Banjee was not frightened by a shadow as she says.

16. I SAW HIM DO IT!

Why does Kelly think the old woman will not be able to see the killing, and that, in fact, "the whole thing is wrong"?
The old woman's glasses will be fogged because she has come into a warm kitchen from the sharp cold outside. Today's optical market offers a coating for sale that prevents fogging in these conditions, but the scene goes to some pains to suggest the time period is reasonably early in the twentieth century, before such material became available. Not only would the woman not be able to see the murder, she wouldn't be able to see anything at all until her glasses cleared. Therefore, "the whole thing is wrong" because none of the shots "through her eyes" would work.

17. A LOGICAL SUSPECT

What evidence has convinced Megan that "Normie was here"?
The plants (daisies, marigolds, and salvia) are all in healthy condition. They must have had the necessary watering at sunset last night, or they would be drooping by this time. Someone had to have activated the generator to provide power for the automated system when the power failure started. If Sonja and her husband were away, Normie was

the only one who could have done so. Therefore, he was at the greenhouse at dusk, when the little girl was taken.

18. TIVERTON VS. CAPELLI

Why does Leona believe there is "no way Tiverton could have seen that wire"?
The accident occurred at the end of October, nine months before Leona's visit to the site in mid-July. The gully is surrounded by thick stands of trees, especially maple. By this time of year, fallen leaves would nearly fill the gully. Both the wire and the ribbons, if they were indeed tied to the wire, would likely have been covered.

19. TREVOR WILKEY'S JOURNAL

What is the "specific reason" Major Gordon refers to?
The lieutenant is guilty of either murder or criminal neglect, for he deliberately or incompetently lost the sextant down a crevasse, and set the compass in a way that sent Captain Wilkey off course. A compass has two arrows: a floating one that always seeks North, and a fixed one that can be rotated. (Some compasses have just one: the floating one.) As any Boy

Scout (and most everyone else) knows, if you know the direction you must travel to reach a point (something you can get from a map or a sextant) and are using a compass, you first allow the floating needle to settle at North. Then, with the floating needle at North, you rotate the fixed arrow to the direction you plan to go. (Or in the case of one-arrow instruments, you simply note your direction relative to the floating arrow.) En route, you check your direction periodically by letting the floating needle find North and making sure you are traveling in the direction of the fixed arrow.

Eby was the one who made the last setting of the compass before the sextant was lost. He was also in the lead most of the time, carrying both the compass and the sextant, so it's possible he had been taking the expedition off course the whole time, as Ahmed had argued.

Perhaps he was just incompetent. But perhaps he has not forgotten Margaret, after all.

20. NEXT DOOR TO THE CHIEF

What evidence leads Tony to believe Mr. Litt planned to come right back home after the dentist visit?

Mr. Litt is obviously precise and organized, almost obsessively so. Yet he left windows open in his office (into which no one else is allowed) on a day when a big storm is predicted. It appears to Tony Morello that Mr. Litt did plan to come home right after the visit to the dentist and the quick errand.

21. A COLUMBO CASE

Doctor Pelowich hands the case back to the police because it's not a suicide. What is the clue that leads him to that conclusion?

The scene is arranged to show the body as a suicide who rigged his car for that purpose and then drove to The Bluffs, parked, and let the car run until he died. Naturally, once he is dead, the car will keep running until it runs out of gas. Doctor Pelowich assesses that the body has been dead for more than a day, based on the way it smells. However, if the man had in fact died in the car from carbon monoxide poisoning more than a day before, the ignition would have drained the battery once the car had run out of gas. In that case, the radio would not have had power to play a classical—or any—station. Doctor Pelowich concludes, therefore, that the car, with the body already inside, was transported up to The Bluffs more recently by someone who set the scene to look like a suicide.

22. THE CHASE

Why does Finn believe "the old guy lied"?
The old man said he had just come up the hill himself, and noted the truck passing and then taking the left fork. The hill is very long and steep. If an old man with a large stomach had just come up such a hill, he would be puffing, or at least breathing hard. He would not be able to stand so casually (drawing a long sigh) and communicate in the way he does.

23. THE KEY TO THE CODE

On what evidence does the last speaker base his theory that "this guy is gone for days, maybe longer"?
The "guy" whose studio or office is being searched is apparently obsessive about arranging and organizing his things, especially his books. While one searcher was looking into the computer, the other was going through the books, calling out the author and title of several different subject sections. All of these were called out in alphabetical order (by author, as they are shelved in a library, whether it uses the Dewey or the Library of Congress system) except Frederick's book on day hikes in Yellowstone. This searcher concludes that since the Frederick book is out of order in an obsessively ordered alphabetical shelving system, the "guy" has been using it to prepare for some hiking in Yellowstone, across the country from where they are now.

24. ONE CLEAR SHOT

D'Arcy Jerome knows that Frith will be shooting at an angle. Why, if the ships are identical, will this be necessary?
The identical ships, the Star of Mombasa and Star of Mandalay, are coal-burning steamships, as were all passenger liners at the time of Queen Victoria's jubilee (the end of the nineteenth century). When the Mombasa arrives in Bombay, it will have used up almost all of its coal. The Mandalay is about to sail for England, so its fuel holds will be fully loaded. Thus, even though the ships are identical and docked side by side, and even though Rodney's and Agatha's rooms will be directly opposite each other, the arriving ship will be riding very high in the water and the departing one very low. (A typical liner of the day would ride as much as four or five feet higher after burning three to four hundred tons of coal on an ocean crossing.) Rodney will have to fire down into Agatha's stateroom at a fairly steep angle, which potentially makes her a more difficult target.

25. BLANK WITNESSES

Marni Dreyfuss feels that being a woman has given her an edge in figuring out that Mrs. Wilson has lied to her. What part of Corinne Wilson's story does not ring true to her?
Marni does not accept that Mrs. Wilson had her back to number 15 because she was going across the lawn to get a sheet of old newspaper.Mrs. Wilson acknowledges that she was outside at the time, and that she may have seen the Fawcetts briefly. Numbers 15 and 17 are to the left of her house, the direction of the sidewalk in front of each house that eventually leads to the alley. To go to the right after the offending sheet of newspaper, and then on down between her house and the Taylors' at 21, Corinne Wilson would have

had to go across her lawn. As Mr. Gomes indicates, there is a heavy dew on this fall morning. Mrs. Wilson, dressed early for her meeting, is most definitely not the type of woman who would cross a wet lawn in open-toed suede shoes.

26. "FOR WANT OF A NAIL ..."

What is the glitch that has ruined this "perfect crime"?
T.G. had instructed Turgeon to come up with a "fresh scoop" and to choose a vehicle that will not attract attention. Turgeon stole the car that very morning, and a green Honda Civic is common enough to fulfill the second requirement. But it is way too small to transport twenty million dollars in used tens and twenties.

The trunk and interior of this car has approximately 96 cu. ft. of available space. That is slightly less than the volume of twenty million dollars evenly split between used twenties and tens. To be able to drive, an adult needs about 16 cu. ft. The two passengers, whom T.G. will not be able to leave behind, together will need about 20 cu. ft. They may still get away with about half the loot, but for want of a larger vehicle they will lose about ten million dollars. The glitch in T.G.'s perfect plan is that he did not tell Turgeon to steal a van or similar vehicle. Perhaps her tight shorts took up too much of his attention.

27. ONE WAY TO BREAK UP A GLOOMY DAY

Mary Margaret is right. Why could this not have been a "failed brakes affair"?
The accident could not have been a brake failure unless Melnick's truck is able to defy gravity by rolling uphill. Mary Margaret's desk faces west. She cranes left to watch the sun set over the park, so the hallway wall her desk touches must

be on her right, or north. The furniture store is next door (also north) and Melnick's store is across the road and two doors further north. The slope of the street is downhill toward Melnick's, because that's the direction the McDonald's wrapper floated in the gutter. Quite rightly, Mary Margaret believes the old truck was deliberately accelerated. If its brakes had failed, it would have rolled away from the furniture store and her office.

28. A PERFECT WITNESS

What has Serena noted that may weaken Father Belcher's value as a witness?
Father Belcher is near-sighted. He wore his glasses coming into Serena Gelberg's office and put them on again as he left. But he read a portion of the police report without putting them on. If the defense discovers that he reads without glasses on and wears them at all other times, they will use the fact that he was reading his "office" when the accident happened to cast doubt on whether he could see well enough—in fading light and from across the street—to determine that a young girl wearing a "peculiar little necklace" got out of the accident car.

29. ACCIDENTAL DEATH?

Why does the insurance company not regard Mr. Lutz's death as "accidental" for insurance purposes?
Mr. Lutz fired first—twice—and therefore the company regards him as "provocative" in the situation. If he died instantly of a bullet to the heart, he had to have fired first.

30. IT'S ELEMENTARY

What elementary clues did Watson miss that point to Hank Lipsett's likely innocence in this shooting? (There are at least three.)

The boot tracks that lead from Hank Lipsett's barn to the spot along the fence where the shooter stood are sunk quite deep into the snow, so they must have been made late in the day, after the surface had been well softened by the sun. (In the weather conditions Watson describes, the snow would be solid enough to support someone walking on the surface only for the first few hours of daylight.)

Also, Hank Lipsett, who loads his own ammunition, would be unlikely to leave an empty shell casing behind, because a casing can often be reused. Further evidence of Hank's innocence lies in the fact that the shell casing had also sunk into the snow. An hour or two of sunlight would have heated the metal casing to a higher temperature than its immediate surroundings, so that it would melt its way down. Hank, if he visited the spot later in the day, could easily fail to see it, as Watson had.

Domie—and a split-second later, Watson—realized that Hank must indeed have gone to the fence some time after the shooting, just as he said.

31. A SECOND INVESTIGATION AT BEDSIDE MANOR

Freddy has uncovered what he believes to be a scam in the matter of the stolen passports (and money and jewelry). What has his investigation revealed?

Freddy entered the Mill Room and noted through the two windows in the opposite wall that the water wheel was turn ing from right to left, or from where he stood, counterclockwise. When he turned to the right and looked out the picture window, he noted where the stream originated and saw that it flowed toward the mill. If the water flow were moving the wheel, it would be revolving the opposite way, from left to right, or clockwise from Freddy's position. The wheel, therefore, is not being moved by the water in the stream, so it must be moving under electric power.

According to Lawrence, the turning of the gears by the water wheel made enough noise to cover the sound of the thief at work. But there was a power outage at the time, so the electric-powered wheel would not have been turning. Someone, certainly the couple from Moldova, possibly with the collusion of the Bedside Manor's owners, is pulling a scam.(When he got back to the in-laws, Freddy's wife, who taught geography to the seventh grade, told him that Moldova is one of the former Soviet republics, and that it's just south of the Ukraine and east of Romania. He got a great kick out of explaining this to the guys at the precinct.)

32. WAS LAWRENCE REALLY THERE?

How does Perry know the photo has been "patched together"?
In the photograph, the older Lawrence Durban is holding an umbrella over himself and Senator Grant, so it must have been raining. Yet the awning at Durban's store is rolled down. Awnings today are made of synthetic fibers that can resist damage by rain, but until these became available—well after 1938—store-owners, especially "fusspot" types like Lawrence the First, would invariably run to wind them up at the first sign of rain. Canvas is too easily discolored, even damaged, by rain. Perry deduced that the two older men, the younger Lawrence Durban, and the store were all photographed at

separate times, and that the photograph Marsha brought to him had therefore been constructed from separate sources.

33. PERSONAL EFFECTS

Something in the tote bag makes one of the two speakers suspect that Shareef Abu Ibrahim may not have committed suicide. What is it?

Whether or not the prescription of methylphenidate hydrochloride is for Shareef Abu Ibrahim or for someone in his family, he had it filled the day after the "it has failed" e-mail message was sent by his wife in Amman. The message was sent April 26. He had the prescription filled on April 27, the day he is alleged to have shot himself ("four weeks ago today" as one of the speakers says, "today" being May 25). Quite rightly, it seems most illogical to the speaker that someone intending to end his life would bother to go get a prescription filled.

34. THE RANKLED BROTHERS

What is it that "did not make sense" to Kerry?

Kerry notes that the roof on Tommy's side of the house, unlike Simon's, is covered in snow. On a one-story house, snow will gradually melt away from the roof if the house is heated warmly on the inside, as has apparently been the case on Simon's side. However long Tommy has been dead—and that has not yet been determined—there has evidently been no fire in his stove since the last snowfall five days before. Yet Simon says he heard Tommy put wood in his stove the night before last—two full days after the storm. If Tommy had actually had his stove going, the snow on his roof would be gone too.

ABSOLUTELY AMAZING FIVE-MINUTE MYSTERIES

35. A CLEAR CASE OF ARSON

Why is the fire investigator sure that if either of the brothers rode near the gazebo on the day of the fire, it is the other one, not the one she is speaking to?

The rider of the Phrygia bicycle that left tracks by the burned gazebo had to have had significant weight. The tracks are a single set, and one of them (the one that is 47 mm wide) weaves a bit. That would be the front tire. The other tire, the back tire, makes a wider track because a heavier weight is on the seat. If the other brother is trying out for a football team, he must have significantly more weight than the skinny boy playing basketball.

36. THE IRISH PROBLEM

Diogenes Simpson reports that the Papists from the Mount St. Patrick settlement tract are being blamed for the deliberate burning of the Loyal Orange Lodge in Killarney "although it could not be so." Why could they not have done it?

The Papists from Mount St. Patrick could not have made it to Killarney on March 28, two days after the ice broke up and flowed out of the Shan River. There is a twenty-league trip on a canal to get to the Shan, and ice on still water disappears at a much slower rate than that on flowing water. Melting ice on a river flows away on the current. This can't happen on a canal. The canal would be impassable for three to four days or more after the ice flowed out of the Shan River on the twenty-sixth of March.

37. CHOOSING THE RIGHT CLIENT

On what basis has he chosen the client?

Both potential clients have the same identifying characteristics as given by the customer, and both appear to be running an errand at a store they are not familiar with. There is a slight difference between the retail nature of Love 'n' Roses and that of Mae's Gift Shoppe, but not enough, given the vagueness of the customer's instructions, to distinguish one from the other as a flower shop. The clue the shooter picks up on is based on his experience in maximum security. In prisons, especially in "max," prisoners never open a door. Thus they develop the habit of standing at a door and waiting for it to be opened, like the client in front of Love 'n' Roses did.

38. SOMEWHERE IN THE DESERT

What information in the note, combined with what the two officers know, points to the most likely search area?

The two officers now know that Kitty ate breakfast at Red's around 9:00 a.m. Her note—which can be taken as authentic because the names of her goldfish were scrawled at the bottom—says she was kidnapped behind Red's, so that would have to be reasonably close to the same time. Kitty says she was tied and put on the floor behind the seat of what she is ninety percent certain is a black Chevy, and covered with a blanket. Perhaps more important is that she was laid out with her head behind the passenger seat. The man with the cough and hand that smelled of pickle held her head down. The other man, about whom she had no information, drove.

When they traveled along pavement (which Kitty would be able to distinguish from dirt by the sound of the tires—a sound difference even more pronounced in a typical pickup truck), Kitty could see a spot of sunlight shining on her right through the hole in the blanket, so they must have been traveling west out of town. At that time of morning the sun would be in the southeast. When they turned onto a dirt road, the spot of sunlight was toward her feet. Her feet were behind the driver's seat so they must have turned right, or north. Tom, therefore, will choose the area west and north of town as the most likely search area.

39. J.T.C. KAPCHEK'S OPENING LECTURE

What is the failure?

In a crime where circumstantial evidence may be crucial, keeping track of the evidence—and being able to prove that it has not been tampered with between the time of investigation and a possible trial—is equally crucial. That is why the investigators were supplied with two cameras. Although one of the investigators took a very careful and extensive set of photographs, they did not insure against technical failure or other possible lapse by repeating the procedure with the second camera. (It is not uncommon in high-profile crime scene situations for the investigators to wait for film to be developed before modifying the scene. The pair did not do this either.)

40. THE CHAIN OF THE PEOPLE

How did Bin war get the artisans to do it?

He paid the requested fee. There are five clans, each with an equal piece of chain. Since there are twenty links in total, each piece then had four links. It cost one white cirra skin to open a link and close it around another. If an artisan opens a link at one end of a piece of chain and closes it around a link at the end of another piece, he will have to do this five times (at a cost of five skins), since there are five pieces of chain. However, if the artisan opens all four links in one piece of chain and uses them to join the remaining four pieces of chain into one continuous loop, or necklace, it can be done in four operations.